CHRONICLES OF KANE

*"Let your imagination become a gateway
to a whole other world."*

Timothy Aberle

Joshua Tree
Publishing

• Chicago •

CHRONICLES OF KANE
Timothy Aberle

Published by
Joshua Tree Publishing
• Chicago •
JoshuaTreePublishing.com

13-Digit ISBN: 978-1-941049-03-7

Front Back Cover Image Credit: Aberlewest

Disclaimer:

This is a work of fiction. Names, characters, places, and incidents are the product of the author's imagination or have been used fictitiously. Any resemblance to actual persons, living or dead, events, locales or organizations is entirely coincidental. The author and publisher of this book shall have neither liability nor responsibility to any person or entity with respect to any loss or damage caused or alleged to be caused directly or indirectly by the information contained in this book.

Printed in the United States of America

Dedication

*This book is dedicated to my wife,
who without you I would have never had the courage
to see my dreams through and this book would have
stayed trapped in my imagination forever.*

Table of Contents

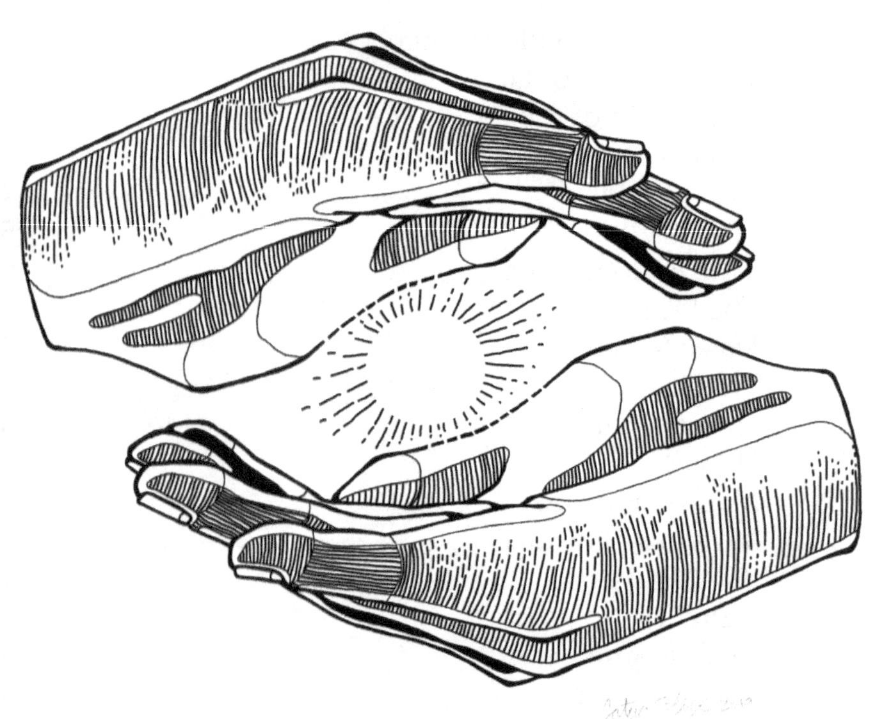

Preface: Creation

Mariam

In the beginning, a star hurtled through space. It was bright, everlasting as the sun. It seemed as if it knew its destination. All around, scattered in different directions were perfect circular rocks called planets, but only one stood out among them all. It had bodies of water all over it that made it blue with hints of green and turquoise. Seeing this beautiful planet, the star picked up speed and, with immense force, hit a sand dune near a body of water, forming a huge crater. Dust flew everywhere. Through the dust, there was a dim light in the shape of a human being standing there. He had long brown hair pulled back into a ponytail and a long light-brown beard. Wearing a long beautiful white cloak with dark-red undergarments, he looked like a wizard, absent a wooden staff. Kneeling down, he picked up a handful of sand, and in the other, he cupped some of the water.

"Well, that's refreshing. A bit salty, but refreshing," he said, talking to himself, sipping the water.

Lifting the sand up to his face, he put it to his lips and gently blew on it and smiled. He combined the water with the sand, and it created a sort of clay. Splitting it up and holding some in each hand, he began swirling his hands around each other gently but never touching one another, and he kept them close to his body. Then he extended his hands out, motioning his hands on either side of each other, shaping his own image as if he were painting on a beautiful canvas. Then a brilliant light appeared, and another being stood before him, slightly different from himself, having white wings. When it opened its eyes, he took its hands into his, and the light softly dimmed. Standing before him now was a beautiful white-skinned, blue-eyed being with long blond hair.

"What am I?" it asked as it smiled and looked down at itself.

"My child, your name is Eden. You are the first of many angels I will create."

"I look different than you. Why?"

"You're beautiful. Just the way I made you. The reason you look different is because you're female. I am male. I have much to teach you, Eden. Watch me and learn. I will show you many beautiful things and what it is to be God."

"Is that your name, God?" Eden asked as he smiled and laughed.

"If that is what you wish to call me, then yes, child. I am God," he said, softly placing his hand gently on her cheek.

After God created Eden, he taught her the importance of understanding mana. Mana was the energy that Orinangels possessed. They could absorb energy from all living things around them. The only beings in existence that could create their own mana were any being directly made from God's loins. This was called Ranin Mana. He also taught Eden the art of creating life. Together, they made the sand they stood on into a beautiful paradise with all different species of beautiful animals, landscapes, all given the means to procreate. They came to call the planet Earth. Eden enjoyed the gifts God gave her. They went on to create more angels—angels of different skin tones, all bearing wings of different shades of color. Eden and the other angels were all given the means to procreate and the gift of a soul. Souls were the angels' identities. They were what gave the angels their free will to forge their own destinies. This soul was a gift from God and Eden, but if God or Eden were to choose to strip that angel of their soul, the angel would cease to be and inevitably die. Angels, like Eden, were beautiful and full of life.

"Let there be life in the sea," God said, looking out over the body of water and raising his hands in the air. "This is called an ocean," he told his angels and Eden as he smiled.

He loved the earth and the peace it gave him so much, so he created another beautiful paradise with his beloved ocean in the clouds above the earth. He called it heaven. Like the earth, he created heaven with all kinds of different species of animals, landscapes, all given means to procreate. Heaven was divided into five realms. Seeing the earth and all he and Eden created, he did not want to leave it uninhabited. He picked up a handful of wet sand from the ocean floor.

"What are you doing?" another angel named Nathaniel asked, watching God.

"Watch carefully, son, and learn. I will show you something beautiful," he said, bringing the wet sand to his lips.

Whispering something, he gently blew on it. Then putting his hands together, he lathered the wet sand all over them. As angels watched, Eden looked and smiled. Walking over to God's side, she did the same. Nathaniel then tried, but he was unable to create. Carefree, he and the other angels stood by and watched God and Eden create human beings.

As time passed, God and Eden were blissfully happy. Nothing made them as proud as when their daughter Everin was born. All of heaven rejoiced and celebrated her birth. However, as time passed, some angels grew to loathe the human beings of the earth and felt that God and Eden possibly loved them more. Angels had always been loyal and loved God and Eden, but through the years, their voices went unheard. Unlike the angels, human beings grew self-centered and worshipped false idols and possessions. Nathaniel, the second angel to be created after Eden, was considered among the wisest of the elder angels. He sought counsel with God and Eden. The elder angels, once known as Orinangels, were of the first angels created and were given the label of "elders" through angels in heaven. The elders and their opinions held much weight with God and Eden. Nathaniel, seeing that human beings had stopped worshiping God, suggested they send the human beings of earth a gift, a savior of their own kin. He explained that through this savior, humans would come together to worship God again. This savior would have god-like powers no different than God himself. He would create a ministry and, through Him, be granted eternal life in heaven. His name would come to be echoed throughout eternity.

"Nathaniel, how would we go about giving them someone of their own?" God kindly asked.

"I have walked among them, Your Highness. Many of them are uneducated when it comes to you, Lord. I volunteer myself to go and see it done. There is a very kind lady among them. She and her husband, Joseph, are God-fearing, and they pray to you often. They are unable to conceive a child of their own, and they would love the child unconditionally. Her name is Mariam Christ," Nathaniel explained. "All I would need, Lord, is your blessing to see it done. The boy would then bear your image among them and know nothing other than how to spread the Word of God and bring people together."

"You would give this boy all the same powers as I?"

"Yes, it would be something that would forever flow through the Christ bloodline."

"I don't know why, but I'm strangely comfortable with it," God said, looking at Eden. "You have my blessing, Nathaniel."

The Son of Man

The rain fell violently on Nazareth. It was the worst storm I had ever seen. I felt as if every bolt of lightning struck me. Roads were closed, and we were warned to stay indoors till the storm passed. As I began to prepare a pot of tea, I heard a knock at the door. Thinking it was Joseph, I opened it. There standing on my doorstep was one of the most handsome men I'd ever seen. He was tall and masculine. The curls of his light-brown wet hair were beautiful. He was stunning. His clothing was like something I'd never seen. He had a worn metal chest plate, black boots with worn metal shin guards, and a gray cloak that sheltered him from the rain.

"Have you traveled far, sir?" I asked politely.

"You have no idea," he said as I took his hand and brought him in out of the rain.

"May I warm myself by your fire, Mariam?"

"Do I know you?" I asked as he took off his cloak.

"Do you believe in God, Mariam?" he then asked, walking over to the fire.

"That's a difficult question."

"No, it's not."

"Who are you?"

"Don't lose faith, Mariam. He believes in you," he said as he walked up to me.

"You can just call me Mary," I said, slowly breathing and becoming nervous as he came close to me.

"You are so beautiful," he said as he placed his right hand on the left side of my cheek. "Do you trust me?"

I don't know why, but I trusted him more than anyone in the world. I thought, *I don't even know him, but I find myself falling in love with him.* When he kissed me, his lips were soft and moist. I felt completely vulnerable to him. Guilt fell over me. I felt like a harlot, but I didn't care. How could I do this to Joseph? Closing my eyes, I envisioned him making love to me. Was he making love to me? I became lost in this dream of pure tranquility. It was beautiful and more real than anything I'd ever imagined.

When I woke the next morning, I was in my bed, completely naked. *Who was that man?* I thought. *Was last night even real?* Suddenly, I felt nauseous. I vomited all over myself and the bed. Getting up, I cleaned up and grabbed my dark-blue cloak. Looking down, I saw my stomach. It had a bulge as if I were pregnant. When I told Joseph, he was so happy and excited. He thought it was his. I thought it was his, but I couldn't be sure. The dream was so real.

"Mary, I thought you couldn't bear children," Joseph said. "Praise God. He has blessed us."

"Indeed, he has, Joseph," I replied softly. "Praise God."

The night the boy was born, every human being was given the gift of a soul. Unlike an angel's soul, a human being's soul was the key to everlasting life. One day when they'd die, they would be granted entrance into heaven. The night of his birth, Nathaniel came to them with a gift. He created a female owl that would serve as a guardian to the boy. She would never leave him, harm him, judge him, or neglect him. She would give her very life to ensure his survival. Her name was Tigist. She had a beautiful coat of brown and black feathers with hints of white throughout. Through the years, Mary could see that Tigist took her role as the boy's guardian very seriously. Mary knew that Tigist possessed supernatural powers, and that she and the boy were as one. However, she also knew that the boy was a gift to the world. He was the Son of God, the Son of Man. His name was Jesus Christ.

***

Jesus

It was early morning in Nazareth. The sun was bright and everlasting. As I opened my eyes, I could feel the warmth of the sun hitting my face. I gently rolled over in bed and looked at her. She was so beautiful. The way the sun lit up all the curves of her nude body, I swear I could see through her, into her soul. All of Nazareth knew her as a thief, a harlot, but they didn't know her as I did. I knew her as Mary Magdalene. She was once a thief and harlot, but no more. She turned from being in that darkness and became part of my flock. When she came to me, she was lost and broken. She learned through me the love of God and became one of my disciples. Though I knew my time was coming to an end, I did what I was destined to do: God's ministry has been created. I brought the Word of God back to the world, and betrayal was now on the horizon. Judas was going to betray me. I could have told my disciples; they would do anything for me, but I didn't. I'd ask myself why at times, but I knew this was how it was supposed to end for me. It didn't mean that I wasn't scared, though. I'd been dreading this my whole life, and thou shalt not kill.

Judas's eyes betrayed him yesterday in the marketplace. That was when I had known for sure of the betrayal. The kiss I received from him on the cheek sealed both our destinies. Mine, without my inevitable death, I would not be able to give salvation to humanity. Judas's, without him, I would not be able to give that salvation. Every step he and I ever took was leading to this. I knew what was going to happen next—forsaken or not. I never expected to fall in love, though. Mary was the most beautiful thing in this world to me, and even in our short time together, she and I lived a lifetime's worth. Gently leaning over, I kissed her for one last time. Our lips together, soft and moist, I embraced her with a hug. I asked God to always watch over her and bless her with all his love.

"Jesus," she softly whispered as she opened her eyes.

"Yes, my love?" I replied.

"I love you, Jesus."

"As I love you, Mary."

Getting up from my bed, I grabbed my tunic from the windowsill, warm from the morning sun blistering down on it, and I draped it around myself. Walking outside, Tigist flew over to me and sat on my shoulder. I remember the first time I heard Tigist speak to me. Through telepathy, she and I have always spoken. One of the greatest memories that I hold dear in my heart was when she first spoke to me. She had always been the voice of reason, my guardian protecting me. Even through my trials and errors, she never judged me. I couldn't help but wonder whether that night, when I dreamed of my death, she saw it too.

"Ah, Tigist, my friend, are you ready for this?" I softly asked.

"Be strong, Jesus. I'll be with you every step of the way," Tigist said, snuggling her cheek up to mine.

I looked down the dusty road leading to my home. I could see the Sanhedrin coming. No doubt they were hired by the high priest Joseph Caiaphas to arrest me, the Son of Man, Jesus. Taking a deep breath as they drew closer, I asked God to give me strength.

"Tigist, go now," I said.

"Are you the one they call, Jesus?" a tall Sanhedrin mounted on a horse demandingly asked when they arrived at my doorstep.

"I am he," I confidently replied. "I know why you've come."

"Jesus, you are hereby arrested by the Sanhedrin. Men, put him in shackles."

"Why? Why are you doing this? Do you know who he is?" Mary replied, running out the house up to one of the Sanhedrin.

"Aren't you the harlot, Mary Magdalene?" one of them sneered.

"Not anymore."

"Not anymore. Once a harlot, always a harlot."

"This does not matter. Take the prisoner!" the tall Sanhedrin demanded.

"Mary, go tell my disciples. Tell them what you've seen here."

After putting shackles on me, I watched as they tied a noose out of rope. They put it around my neck and began to ride back down the dirt road just fast enough for me to walk and keep up. As we walked through Nazareth, I could see Tigist in the sky, hovering just above us. I looked at the temple where I had once expelled merchants and money changers out of. Suddenly, Mark, one of my disciples, came from out of nowhere. Sword in hand, I watched him hit a Sanhedrin I was familiar with named Malchus off his horse. Getting up off the ground, Mark swung his sword again, this time severing Malchus's ear from his head.

"Enough, Mark! Listen to me, this is not the way, my friend!" I yelled, grabbing him before the Sanhedrin could kill him.

"Jesus!" Mark replied with tears filling his eyes. "Forgive me, Jesus."

"Mark, my friend, there is nothing to forgive," I said, lifting his chin and looking him in the eye. "He who believes in me will have salvation. I am the light," I said as Malchus cried in pain from his ear being severed.

"Kill that man!"

"Sir, I beg you to spare his life."

"It's Captain."

"Captain, I beg you to spare his life."

"Look what he has done to one of my men."

I looked over to see two temple guards helping Malchus, who was on his knees in pain. The other three were standing over Mark and I. Standing up slowly with my hands in the air, I slowly walked and picked up Malchus's ear from the ground. Walking up to Malchus, I could still hear Mark sobbing as the Sanhedrin kept their swords pointed at him. As the Sanhedrin watched, I cupped the ear in my hands and put it to my lips, whispered, and gently blew on it.

"Heresy! That warlock will bewitch us!" one of them near Malchus said firmly.

"Quiet you!" the captain said firmly. "Jesus, I warn you, be careful. Now help him," the captain said. As I opened my hands, the ear was gone.

"Don't be scared," I told Malchus, putting my hand up to where his ear once was. Between my hand and his head, a faint green glow began. I took my hand away, and his ear was back.

"What is this? Witchcraft. How did you do that?"

"Let he who has faith walk with me through the gates of heaven."

"Are you really the Son of Man?" Malchus asked, shocked and amazed by my gift.

"Do you not see? He is Jesus of Nazareth. He is the Son of God. You would condemn him?" Mark asked, looking at the Sanhedrin.

"Jesus, I'm sorry, but Son of Man or not, we are under orders. We have to take you, but we do not have to take you like a prisoner. Would you, Jesus, come with us willingly?" the captain asked politely as he removed the noose and unshackled my hands.

"I will," I replied.

"Malchus, where are you going?" the captain asked firmly.

"I can't be part of this anymore. I cannot condemn Jesus of Nazareth," Malchus replied before hugging me. "I believe in you, Jesus."

"Jesus, what are you doing?" Mark asked, confused at my response to go willingly.

"All you need to know, my friend, is that everything is happening the way I have foreseen it. Now go, as Malchus has to tell everyone what you have seen here."

"I will, Jesus," Mark replied, hugging Jesus for the last time.

As I was walking down the road with the Sanhedrin, they asked me many questions about God. I answered their questions the best I could, and they listened to me, intrigued by what I was telling them.

"Jesus, why is it they say you lie?" one of them asked.

"They see only what they wish. I was sent here to all humanity to reveal the Word."

"What is the Word, Jesus?"

"God, he stands for everything pure and good, and he loves you all so much that he sent his only begotten Son to teach you all."

Still scared, I continued walking with the Sanhedrin. I knew the outcome of everything to come. When we reached the walls of Jerusalem, I advised the Sanhedrin to put the shackles back on. I was to be a criminal again. We walked through the streets of Jerusalem; there were people everywhere—the mob, they called it. Some shouted blasphemies while some watched silently, scared to say anything. They took me to the palace of the high priest Joseph Caiaphas.

"Are you the Christ?" Caiaphas firmly demanded.

"Why don't you answer your high priest?" one of the chief priests sneered.

"Are you the Christ!" Caiaphas yelled.

"I am, and you will see me, the Son of Man, firmly seated at the right hand of power and coming on the clouds of heaven," I responded.

"Blasphemy!" a chief priest yelled.

"Jesus, you are hereby charged with blasphemy."

They took me before Pontius Pilate, the Roman governor of Jerusalem. Caiaphas and his chief priests claimed before Pilate that I had broken Mosaic law. I believe that they were hoping that Pilate would deem this as a capital offense by interpreting Roman law. I watched as they failed to convince Pilate. When this did not work to their benefit, they accused me, the Son of Man, of sedition against Rome by opposing the payment of taxes to Caesar and naming myself King. Pilate took my hand and invited me to walk with him in private.

"Why do you take him and not give us justice, Pilate!" Caiaphas yelled.

"Justice? How dare you raise your voice to me," Pilate said in a low but steady tone.

"I apologize, Governor. I meant nothing by it," Caiaphas said, apologizing.

"We shall see," Pilate responded instilling fear in Caiaphas.

Caiaphas and his chief priests, becoming silent and outraged, waited patiently. I watched as Pilate, without saying a word, turned one last time and glared at them.

"Are you the King of the Jews?" Pilate asked, looking at me politely.

"It is as you say," I replied.

"Listen, Jesus, I will tell you honestly. I do not agree with these priests. There is no evil in you, I know this much. You know it to be a custom that at Passover, I have the authority to release one prisoner. I have a criminal named Barabbas. He is a murderer and as evil as they come. I will offer the mob outside that speaks against you to choose either him or you. My hope is they ask for your release over Barabbas."

I was taken to a holding cell where they kept the prisoners—murderers, rapists, thieves. These were of the human beings I was among now.

"Are you the Christ everyone is talking about, the one who calls himself the King of the Jews?" a prisoner in the next cell asked.

"I am he," I responded.

"I'm a bad man, Jesus. I've robbed and killed. You don't belong here with us."

"My son, God sends me to those who are in need."

"Jesus, I've been a terrible person."

"Do not worry. I forgive you, and soon, I will take you to heaven with me."

"You would do this?"

"Those who repent for their sins will never be forgotten."

I heard the mob outside, grow angrier and louder. I knew my time was limited when a Roman guard came and escorted Barabbas and I to the mob. Barabbas lashed out at the soldier like a wild animal. As we walked down the narrow hall, I took a deep breath and looked around till we walked through a doorway. When I saw the mob yelling blasphemies, I looked out among them with no fear. I saw my disciples, but more importantly, I saw Mary with Tigist perched on her shoulder. Looking at her, she smiled, pointing at her stomach with tears of happiness in her eyes, mouthing the words "We've been blessed." At that moment, I knew my chronicle, my legacy and supremacy would live on through another. When Pilate raised his hand, the mob went silent.

"During Passover, it is customary to release a prisoner. I have two prisoners here—Barabbas, a known murderer and rapist, then Jesus, the King of the Jews." The crowd without hesitation demanded the release of Barabbas.

"Crucify, Jesus!" the mob shouted.

"What evil has he done?" Pilate shouted back.

"Crucify him!" the mob again shouted.

"All you want is blood. I will have no part of this. I am innocent of this man's blood." Pilate washed his hands with water in front of the mob. "I am sorry, Jesus," Pilate said, looking me in the eye.

"I forgive you. My kingdom is not of this world. I came into the world to bear witness to the truth, and all who are on the side of truth listen to my voice."

"What is truth, Jesus?" Pilate replied.

"My ministry on earth is complete. Those who believe in me will have eternal life. I will walk amongst this world again. My bloodline, does not end here—that is truth. Now give the mob what they want. Crucify me, the Son of Man, the Nazarene."

"You don't lie, Jesus. This I know." Pilate nodded and paused. "Crucify him!" Pilate gasped and shook his head in upset.

When the Sanhedrin grabbed my arms, I could feel their fear with the order they had been given to carry out. I felt all the pain. I felt blades ripping at my skin from a whip that was wielded by someone with much hatred in their veins; it was not long before they had me hauling the cross I was to be nailed to through the streets of Jerusalem. When I fell, my sweet Mary ran up to me, patting my face down to get the blood and sweat from my eyes. I saw Tigist fly down and land on the top of my cross.

"Jesus, I love you," Mary said, weeping. "Jesus, you will live on. Everything you are does not end here. There is another," Mary said, sobbing before being pulled away.

I mustered up the strength to carry on till I reached Golgotha. This was to be my final resting place. When they drove the nails in, I saw Tigist fall from the sky.

"Please, Father, forgive them, for they know not what they do!" I yelled as they raised my cross in the air.

Looking at the crowd in front of me that mourned what was to come, I saw Mary pick Tigist up from the ground. Holding her close, Mary looked at me and mouthed, "I believe in you."

"Jesus, where's your God now?" one of the criminals being crucified yelled.

"Jesus, please forgive me. Will you remember to take me to heaven with you?" the criminal I had met earlier in the cell humbly asked, gasping.

"Yes, he who believes in me will have everlasting life. Tigist, we did it. Our ministry on earth is complete. We can leave this place now."

I looked at Mary and Tigist one last time, and I looked to the sky. Closing my eyes gently, I felt my head become heavy, and everything became dark. Suddenly, gray clouds covered the sun, and it began to rain.

The captain of the Sanhedrin who arrested Jesus was then ordered to puncture a spear into his side, below the ribs, to make sure he was dead. When the Sanhedrin lifted it and pierced Jesus, thunder and lightning came crashing down, hitting right through the temple Jesus once evicted all the merchants out of. Mary watched as the life in Tigist left, and she disappeared from Mary's arms.

"Be free, Tigist," Mary whispered.

Though Jesus died on that unholy day, his ministry was complete. The spear that pierced his side became a holy relic known as the Spear of Destiny. The Captain who'd pierced Jesus kept the spear and fled the Roman Empire, and disappeared from existence. Many went searching for it, but they never found it. Among the relics was the Whip of Kismet. Rumors surfaced that after the death of Christ, the Roman who'd wielded the whip on Christ was not a Roman or human at all, but something else entirely.

Governing the Elder Angels

As decades passed in heaven, God called upon the elder angels to take on the responsibilities of ruling heaven. The five realms were to have an elder governing over them. God told the elders that he was aware of some angels flying down from heaven and playing dirty tricks on human beings because of their hatred toward them. This was to be the reason why the realms needed to start being governed. With this said, God cursed and forbade any angel or elder from ever leaving heaven without his blessing.

"I know that human beings have grown very self-centered, arrogant. They have even gone on to worship false idols. However, when their souls come here, we need to welcome them with open arms no matter how damaged they may be. I'm of the idea to create a place that will serve as a rehabilitation; where more-damaged souls may go to seek counsel and heal," God told the elder angels at his home in the courtyard around an emerald green table.

"My Lord, when will you create this place?" Nathaniel asked.

"My friends, it has already begun. I have called upon you, my elder angels, because you four are the oldest and most knowledgeable. My wish is that the four of you will rise to a higher calling and govern these realms."

"Four elders and this new realm you speak of would make five realms, my Lord. Who'd be the fifth governor?" Maya asked.

"My daughter, Everin, will come to govern one of these realms. With you four, she will now make five."

"My Lord, she is but a novice. Inexperienced in such a matter," Roquin said. "Forgive me for saying."

"Watch your tongue when you speak of the princess, Roquin," Nathaniel stood up and said firmly.

"My Lord, I mean no harm toward Everin. I'm just implying that this seems like a position for an angel more qualified," Roquin said glaring at Nathaniel.

"You are no more qualified than I, Roquin," a female voice said from the shadows of the courtyard they sat in.

"Your Highness," Nathaniel said, bowing his head.

As all the elders bowed their heads in respect to the princess, the beautiful young angel walked out from the shadows. She had long black hair that had a gorgeous shine to it when hit by the moonlight. She had beautiful white skin that looked soft and nurturing to the touch. She had blue eyes that anyone could tell she inherited from her mother. She was convincingly confident and ready for anything. As the elders looked at her, one of them could not help but fall deeply and dangerously in love with her.

"Nathaniel," Everin said politely and smiled putting her hand out.

"Everin," Nathaniel responded, nodding and taking her hand gracefully.

"My friends, I stand before you, asking that you now rise to a higher calling and become more than what you are. Become governors of the realms. Elders, allow my mother and father to see what we can do as governing angels ruling over the realms. Do you answer the call, Elders?"

"My place has always been at your father's side, Everin. I humbly accept the gracious offer of becoming a governor," Nathaniel happily said as he continued to stand with Everin. Then one at a time, each of the elders stepped forward, standing next to Everin. They took their places to become governors.

"You will all be given god-like powers to govern. These god-like powers will be passed to you. They will enhance your skills in mana. Things you might have struggled with before will become much easier for you. During the event of your inauguration in which all angels and souls alike will bear witness, you will be given an additional gift," God said, letting the elders know of the event that will take place.

"I don't know how to feel about this," Nathaniel said, nervous and confused.

"Nathaniel, you are ready for this. You've been ready," God said as everyone began walking out of the courtyard together.

"That much power, Lord. We would be your equal."

"Not quite, son, but just about. My only equal, well, you know who that is," God said as he smiled and looked over at Everin.

"Maya, are you excited or what? God-like powers. I always wondered what it'd be like to be God," Lucifer said as he and Maya walked together. "I know Nathaniel is trying to talk God out of it right now."

"Of course he is. Nathaniel always has our best interest in mind, especially God's and I'm sure he doesn't share the same feelings as you on God-like powers."

"Why is that do you think?"

"He believes that no one but maybe Christ should be equal to God."

"Nathaniel's a complicated angel. Of course it'd be him to turn down the world, if it were offered to him."

"Tell me about it."

***

In the months leading to the inauguration ceremony, the elders were highly trained in the arts of fencing, mixed martial arts, self-defense, and Ranin Mana. These were all taught to them by God. Ranin Mana is the ability to use mana at will without having to absorb energy. Of the five elders, only two of them proved to be more lethal with Ranin Mana than any. Lucifer and Everin would now face off in combat. They were to fight each other, and the winner would move on to engage in combat with God himself.

"I felt the coldness of hate come over me. As Lucifer and Everin faced each other, I tried to fight it, but I couldn't help it. All I could think of was Everin and I being together on a physical level. I lusted over her, and the thought of Lucifer even touching her made the skin crawl from my bones. She was mine—her perfect breasts, that perfect body. Nothing else compared to the high I would feel when she would even touch my arm, but I felt guilty for these thoughts. How could I, an elder angel, have such lustful thoughts?

I knew how competitive Lucifer was. He would not back down from anyone. The hate inside me was fierce, and for a moment, I wished death upon Lucifer and made a pact with myself that if he were to get the upper hand over her I would kill him."

When the fight started, Lucifer came at her fast and from out of nowhere. Hurtling through the air, he came down at Everin with a power punch, making full contact with her face, and she fell to the ground. He stood over her and extended his hand out to help her to her feet. When she flew up in the air and threw a kick, landing it right across his face, he fell back. Losing his balance, but only for a moment, he stayed on his feet. With his lip bleeding, he looked at her with a very proud but surprised smile. Fully engaging each other in combat, they moved fast, lunging at each other, both dodging and blocking many punches and kicks. Soon, Everin grappled Lucifer and took him to the ground, putting him in an arm bar. Tapping her leg, he submitted. God stood up with the elders joining him. They congratulated Everin on the victory.

"How are you?" Everin asked, helping Lucifer to his feet.

"I'm fantastic. So long as you know I took it easy on you." Lucifer chuckled and smiled.

"Sure," Everin said, smiling.

"You all have done amazing. I'm proud of you all," God said, shaking his head and smiling till he suddenly placed his hand on his head and gasped.

"What is it, Father?" Everin asked concerned.

"I'm not sure. I just felt a great amount of pain all of a sudden," God said, looking at all his elders. "Forgive me, Elders. Everin, I must go now and see your mother."

***

It was early morning, and the sun was bright. Human souls were everywhere, mingling with angels and one another. Gathering into a larger courtyard at God's home, they gazed upon the balcony. It was a sight to see brick-and-mortar pillars. Perched at the top of each one of them, circling around the courtyard, was a gargoyle.

"God always told us that gargoyles ward off evil, but this couldn't be true what he told us. If they ward off evil, why in this courtyard do I still have impure thoughts of Everin? To be lusting over God's one and only daughter has to be forbidden. I wonder what she'd say if I told her of my desires," this is what I thought about when walking up the stairs in God's home, I saw the curtains that separated us from being presented to all of heaven as governors. I looked through a crack between the wall and the curtain. I saw thousands of human souls and angels. God and Eden were both out on the balcony, talking to all of heaven, telling them of the wonderful things that were going to be happening.

"With all the change that's coming, I found myself calling on the elders, and they have answered the call," God shouted to all of heaven.

"What do you think of Everin joining us?" Roquin asked Nathaniel behind the curtain.

"My opinion doesn't matter. If it's God's will, then it shall be done. She's the princess."

"I know, but the thought of a female angel in charge of anything, it's nerve-racking."

"Are these your thoughts toward Maya also?"

"I mean no disrespect, Nathaniel."

"What's Lucifer doing over there, peeking out from the curtain?" Nathaniel asked Roquin as they stood there. "Lucifer!"

"Gentlemen," Lucifer responded. "How are you both on this fine morning?"

"Damn, Lucifer, what's with the bullets of sweat? You nervous?"

"Very."

"Don't worry, it'll be over soon."

"Now to answer your questions," Nathaniel said, turning to Roquin, "the princess and Maya are just as capable as us to take on this responsibility. You need to show respect."

"I stand corrected, Nathaniel."

"Nathaniel, I need to speak with you," Eden said, gently interlocking her arm with his and walking away from the group.

"My Queen?"

"With this glorious day upon us, Nathaniel, of the elders, are you not the wisest?"

"My Queen?" I asked, confused.

"God and I trust you more than anyone. Which is why we are asking you of the elders who are going to become governing angels, 'Would you, Nathaniel, lead, and guide them?'"

"My Queen, while being honored with this gracious offer, I must decline. I believe no angel is of you or the Lord's equal. It would be better to place the princess in such a position."

"I am but an angel as well, Nathaniel."

"You're much more than that, Your Highness."

"Tell me, Nathaniel, would you help guide Everin?"

"With all my heart, yes. There's nothing I wouldn't do to ensure that she is successful."

"Then it's time, Nathaniel, to take your place amongst the governing angels."

"My Queen, I thank you for the faith you have in me. I will do what I can to help Everin so that she is successful," I said as the Queen walked up the stairs to the balcony.

"What was that all about?" Lucifer asked as he saw Eden and I speaking.

"You will know soon enough, my friend," I responded.

"My children, the elders are amongst you every day. Their business has always been to help heaven flourish. I present to you Maya," God announced to heaven.

When Maya walked out from behind the dark-red curtain, she looked beautiful with long light-brown hair and a slender but toned physique. Standing five-four, she was wearing silver-plated armor with a white tunic draped over her shoulders. Tunics were traditional for elder angels to wear. Embracing Maya with a hug and smile as a father would toward a daughter, he was truly proud of her. God then gently placed his hand on the side of her face. She closed her eyes, and suddenly, her body convulsed. When God gently pulled his hand away from her body, it followed until suddenly the bond released. As all of heaven looked on in amazement, Maya's eyes stayed shut. God turned to all of heaven. In his hand, there was a faint purple glow. This was a piece of Maya's soul. Turning his hand sideways with the soul, he gently blew on it and whispered. Suddenly, to all of heaven's surprise, a katana appeared in God's hand. All of heaven was still looking on in amazement when Maya opened her eyes.

"My gift to you, Maya," God said, handing Maya the beautiful katana. "You and the katana are as one. As long as the katana is in existence, your soul will never perish. It's called the Pater."

God named off the governing angels one by one and presented them all with special katanas that their very souls were infused within. All the katanas had names. Lucifer received the Filius. Roquin received the Geist.

When God performed the ceremony on Everin, her katana was named the Nevillin. It had an angelic sigil etched in the blade, stating the prophecy of Spraygin on one side of the blade and on the other Enreal. God knew Spraygin to mean "the guardian." The name Enreal was the name elder angels referred to Christ in. Enreal means "savior." When it came time for Nathaniel to be recognized by God, something odd happened. When God took a piece of Nathaniel's soul, it came out in the shape of an owl. All of heaven rejoiced when seeing this, looking at it as a good omen. Nathaniel was received by the citizens as heaven's champion. Of all the governing angels that day, the two that stood out among the inauguration were Nathaniel and Everin.

"A champion truly," God said as he embraced Nathaniel with a hug and smile. "Never have I been so proud, Nathaniel. Here is your katana. It's called the Trinity."

"You knew about Tigist?"

"I knew if I taught you to create animal life, you'd give Christ a familiar."

"Nathaniel, when the people of Jerusalem crucified my Son, Tigist returned to you, and there she'll stay till she's needed once more. Earth has not seen the last of my Son, for he will return and bring the righteous to heaven on a cloud of wonders. I'm proud that you left my Son a protector, Nathaniel," God smiled looking sad. "Jesus was blessed to have her."

"How did you know of Christ's death?"

"I felt it. Do remember when Everin and Lucifer faced each other in combat."

"I remember you becoming light headed."

"That was the moment Jesus died. The pain I felt that day was his and it took a toll on me."

"What do you mean it took a toll on you, Lord?"

"Love Maya, every day Nathaniel. Never let your heart stray from her," God said before embracing Nathaniel with a hug.

All the elder angels were able to self-consume their katanas, being that their katanas were an extension of themselves. All the katanas were unique and beautiful, and they all knew nothing but good. God told them that if ever their katanas would be called upon to do evil, the elder would lose the ability to consume their katana.

On this glorious day, God created a grimoire. This grimoire was called the Elder Grimoire. Its purpose was to house all the elders' history and events. The first elder to write in this grimoire was Nathaniel, documenting Christ's sacrifice, the rise of the elder angels, and their fellowship and the prophecy upon the Nevillin, of Spraygin and Enreal.

The Creation of Hell

As centuries passed, peace in heaven reigned. The elder angels ruled over the realms. Though Everin was, in fact, the acting general to the elders, it was Nathaniel whom she had the utmost confidence in. She regarded his opinion above all others. Of course, this didn't remain as an angel claiming to be a prophet began to make claims and create hysteria among the realms. His claims were that all the elders, except Everin, were corrupt. He'd tell story's of how the elders would use intimidation tactics as a way of ruling and abused their authority. He was sophisticated when speaking of heaven's purity and sought to wage rebellion against the elders and create a dictatorship under Everin. His name was Rylin. He had white skin and shoulder-length brown hair that was always combed to the side and pulled back into a ponytail. He was tall and masculine. His eyes were honest and trustworthy. Among the elders, no one despised Rylin more than Nathaniel. Rylin even went to great lengths to seek an audience with God and Eden.

"My Lord, I come to you as a humble servant," Rylin said, barging into a room where God and Eden would often meet with the elders in their home.

"I'm familiar with your antics, Rylin," God said.

"My Lord, if you would just listen," Rylin said before getting cut off.

"Listen to you? You are out there every day speaking out against your elders," God said calmly. "To speak out against an elder is to speak out against me," God paused. "Is that what you're doing, Rylin, speaking out against me?"

"Father, he doesn't question you. He just wants to be heard." Everin said walking into the room.

"Everin."

"Father, may I speak with you and mother alone?" Everin asked.

"You may," Eden replied as the three of them walked into another room.

"Father, you must hear Rylin out, angelic law states."

"Don't verse me, young lady, on angelic law. I wrote it," God said firmly.

"I understand keeping the order, but you can't take away his freedom of speech. You taught us all to be of sound mind, and it says it right there in the grimoire where you wrote the angelic law."

"I understand, Everin. I will hear what he has to say. You're right," God said as they walked back into the room to find Rylin gone.

"I've spoken to many of the angels and souls of the other realms, but every time I have come to speak to you, wonderful citizens . . ." Rylin was speaking as a group of citizens began to form in Nathaniel's realm.

"False prophet, leave our realm!" a female citizen shouted in anger.

"Nathaniel has brainwashed you all and has spoken out against your prophet."

"Our prophet! Who are you that we should listen? There is only one champion here, Rylin, and you are not, he!" an angel shouted as more citizens began to listen.

"And no doubt that champion of yours will be made aware of my presence here very soon. So I ask, 'Why do you think he silences me? Could it be because he is keeping truths from being revealed?'" Rylin shouted out to the citizens of the realm.

"Leave, false prophet! You're not welcome here!" Citizens began shouting.

"That's enough, Rylin!" Everin shouted, hovering above the crowd.

"Your Highness," Rylin responded softly.

"Rylin, come with me now before Nathaniel comes, or there will be trouble."

"Let him come and silence me."

"Rylin, I care about you, but what you're doing . . ." Everin was saying before a deep voice interrupted.

"I thought you were told to never return here, Rylin?" Nathaniel said firmly.

"Well, if it isn't the great, fearless Nathaniel. Mr. judge, jury, and executioner himself."

"You may have many citizens fooled, but you don't fool me, Rylin."

"Nathaniel," Everin said.

"Your Highness."

"You have your katana in hand. I might ask what you're doing."

"I have spoken to Rylin about returning here and the consequences that would come if he did."

"Nathaniel, stand down," Everin said as Nathaniel ground his teeth and grasped his katana tightly. "Nathaniel, stand down now!" Everin repeated firmly.

"The great Nathaniel, silenced by a woman," Rylin said as Nathaniel suddenly swung his katana at Rylin till it was met by another.

"Nathaniel, we are not doing this," Everin begged, holding his katana in place with her own.

"How can you allow him to deceive us . . . to deceive you?" Nathaniel said, disappointed.

"You're wrong, Nathaniel," Everin said shaking her head.

"For all our sakes, I hope I am. I'll do what I must to ensure the safety of my realm, Your Highness. As for you, Rylin, step out of line again, and I will see to it that you meet your end," Nathaniel said, removing his katana from Everin's and pointing it at Rylin. "My apologies, Your Highness, for raising katanas with you."

"There is nothing to apologize for, old friend," Everin said as she smirked at Nathaniel and Rylin flew off.

"There is nothing more to see, citizens. Go back to your lives," Nathaniel said to the angels and souls that just bore witness to what happened.

"May God bless you, Nathaniel!" a voice shouted out over the crowd.

"Nathaniel, we love you. You are and always will be our champion!" another voice shouted as they all began to chant his name together.

"My friends, I appreciate all your love, and it is a blessed day, indeed, for the princess has come to visit us," Nathaniel said as he bowed in respect of the princess.

"Way to change our conversation," Everin said, smiling. "Thank you, my friends," Everin said to the crowd, still smiling.

"I will never understand why you're standing up for Rylin or protecting him."

"He has a big mouth, Nathaniel, I'll give you that. But we enforce angelic law, and Rylin is within his rights. Will I see you at the gathering tonight?"

"I would never miss the gathering, Your Highness," Nathaniel said as he smiled at Everin. "I'll be there."

Fellowship gatherings are what they were called. They took place once a year in heaven. All of heaven would join together and celebrate and rejoice in honor of God. There would be music and all kinds of fun for humans and angels to partake in. All sorts of different food and delicious desserts would be provided. Beverages consisted of anything from tropical fruit drinks for kids to alcoholic drinks for the adults. It was the one time of the year where God would partake in the pleasures of having a drink. His favorite was an aged merlot. He would often say how talented the humans were for having created such a fine drink. It was also the time of the year when the elders would convene in God's home and discuss important matters of heaven.

That night in God's home, Nathaniel suggested all realms deny Rylin the right of speaking out against them. Nathaniel told them that he viewed Rylin's antics as blasphemy and treason and to insult the elders is to insult God himself. He also spoke of the many souls that were coming to heaven more damaged than ever and that these same souls are the reason for many of heaven's problems.

"Elders, I don't disagree with what Nathaniel has said. I do believe that we have a serious issue with the souls we have been receiving," Everin said, walking over next to Nathaniel.

"What do you suggest, Your Highness?" Lucifer asked.

"I would suggest that we look to my father to create a place where these souls can be counseled by us. We can help them, get to know them, and then maybe we'll understand them. We will call this place the abyss. The soul, when the governor deems fit, will be given a second chance at life. Reincarnation is what we will call this."

"Everin, this abyss you speak of, it's a bad idea. Harnessing that much evil and sadness in one spot and trying to contain it is reckless and dangerous."

"Your Highness, I must agree with Nathaniel. This sounds very dangerous," Maya said in agreement.

"We study them, we counsel them, and as a last resort, we execute them if need be," Nathaniel said sternly.

"You would condemn a broken soul to execution?" Maya said, confused.

"For the greater good, why not?"

"Elders, you've heard Nathaniel. What do you say?" Everin asked.

"I'm in agreement with Nathaniel on this, Your Highness," Lucifer said.

"I'll seek counsel with my parents."

"We're not executioners," Maya added.

"Our place has always been at your side, Your Highness," Roquin said, looking at Everin. "We'll trust your lead and guidance."

***

Not before long, the elders watched the creation of the abyss. God reached out to space, taking the brightest star he could find and called it the morning star. He held it in his hands and told us how the stars came to be. Continuing to hold the morning star, he reached down to the darkest part of his beloved ocean, pulling from it an oyster. Handing it to Lucifer, God told him to gently blow on it. After doing so, Lucifer opened it, revealing a black pearl.

"This is odd. I've never seen a black pearl. They're always white," Lucifer said confused by its color.

"It's an omen," God told the elders.

Elders were granted the right to become the judges, the juries, and the executioners of the abyss. Nathaniel spent much of his time in the abyss. Among all the elders, he had the most success with counseling souls and understanding the tortured ones. He granted many of them the blessing of reincarnation. As God's role in heaven seemed to diminish, Everin took on more responsibility than ever with Nathaniel always close by to help guide her. Through the decades, Nathaniel and Maya fell deeply in love. Their union was blessed by God and it filled his heart with such blissful joy to see them happy.

Among the elders, there was one who began to understand the evil that dwelled in the abyss. Having become consumed with hidden hate toward humans and a lust for God's power, this elder became completely consumed by the evil and darkness. The elder learned to harness that evil and use it to its advantage. Becoming more powerful than any other elder, it began down its new hateful path of becoming God himself and only hate began to flow through its veins. This elder forged a new katana in the fires of the abyss. The katana was driven by violence and with its elder came to murder many souls and angels in silence. With every murderous act, the elder began to transform into a god of pure evil and began to make plans of its own.

Remaining devious in its acts, the elder waited for the opportune moment to strike and take heaven by force. This elder created in secret an army of beings that were half angels and half humans, using the tortured human souls of the abyss as the prototypes to infuse and create a being fueled by violence. It even murdered animals and angels and infused them with humans, creating all sorts of monsters fueled with brutality that could run and fly. This army became known as, Jinn. The Jinn were intelligent and would appear as scorching smokeless fire, but they were also physical in nature, which made them susceptible to death. They had the ability to shape-shift and mimic any host it comes in contact with. Some Jinn became responsible for deceiving human beings among nations, causing genocidal attacks. Most notable among the Jinn were Napoleon Bonaparte and Adolf Hitler.

It wasn't till a Jinn in Saudi Arabia changed a great many things when he began referring to himself as a prophet from God. He preyed on weak-minded human beings. He recruited them to fight a war that he would wage on the entire world, forming a new religion. In his name, they unleashed unspeakable attacks and preached hate among the nations. From out of the ashes of his death, terror groups formed in his name and began their attacks, pushing their newfound religion onto the world. They attacked all nations and anyone who did not believe in their prophet. Being able to shape-shift also gave them the ability to deceive heaven and carry out malicious evil deeds. It was not before long that war was witnessed in heaven.

A strong cloud cover came over the gathering the following year; lightning struck, and rain began to pour relentlessly. It only took a couple of minutes before the rain had made huge puddles and streams of water.

"What is this?" Lucifer said, looking to the sky, confused.

"This is bad," Nathaniel added.

"Nathaniel, don't jump to conclusions," Everin said.

"This isn't anything good," Roquin said nervously.

"What's that noise?" Maya said after hearing what sounded like a banshee cry.

Suddenly, from out of nowhere, a devilish creature unlike anything they had ever seen jumped on Lucifer and began trying to tear at his flesh with its claws and teeth. Nathaniel, running to his aid, flicked his wrist when one of these monsters then jumped on him. Stabbing it through the chest, Nathaniel pushed its lifeless body off him. Maya ran to help Lucifer, hitting the monster off him, and it turned into a thin black smoke and disappeared. Maya, helping Lucifer to his feet, gathered with the elders and rushed to get God and the citizens of heaven to shelter.

"My Lord, what is this?" Maya asked God.

"This is nothing I've ever seen before," God said as he engaged one of the devilish things.

"We are Jinn. We've come to take what's yours, and we will do it by any means necessary," one of the devilish things said in a malicious voice as it stared at God.

"You can try, creature," God said, grabbing the thing by its throat and throwing it to the ground.

"Your heaven is coming to an end, and you'll watch it burn along with your precious children. Mark my words: you will watch it burn and not be able to do anything about it," the Jinn said before God snapped its neck.

Fellowship of the Elders

When the sixth realm of heaven was attacked by an army of Jinn, the elder Roquin was ambushed. Standing tall and valiant, he fought the Jinn till his last breath. When the elders arrived in the sixth realm to give assistance, they saw a dark entity drag Roquin's lifeless body away into the darkness.

As Everin hovered in the sky, looking down on what used to be a paradise of wonders, she saw hundreds of Jinn everywhere. This once beautiful place was now reduced to ashes. Everin gave the order to attack the Jinn and take heaven back, but the elders knew it was too late. There were too many casualties. Suddenly, Everin saw a sharp primitive weapon flying toward her, but she was not quick enough. Hitting her left wing, she let out a ghastly cry and began to fall from the sky. She felt numb all over. Then suddenly, she was no longer falling; Nathaniel had caught her.

"Nathaniel?" she said softly.

"I've got you, love," Nathaniel replied.

"Why is this happening?"

"I don't know. I have to get you out of here."

"You mustn't leave, Nathaniel!" Everin demanded as Nathaniel let her go.

"The realm is lost, Everin! We must leave. Now!" Nathaniel shouted.

"I will not let the realm fall!" Everin said pushing herself off Nathaniel.

"It already has! Give us the order to fall back!" Nathaniel firmly demanded.

"I will not give that order!" Everin yelled.

"One last time, Everin. Give us the order!" Nathaniel demanded.

"No!" Everin shouted.

"Then you have sentenced us to death!" Nathaniel shouted in frustration. "Elders! Draw back! Now!"

"This is insubordination!" Everin yelled.

"These are our lives," Nathaniel said, grinding his teeth and getting in her face. "They're not yours to meddle with. I will be taking this matter up with your father," Nathaniel said, turning to fly away.

It wasn't long before Nathaniel went to seek an audience with God to vent his concerns about the reckless behavior he witnessed from Everin in the sixth realm.

***

Nathaniel

As I flew across heaven and looked at God's home from a distance, an eerie feeling came over me. The weather was cloudy and gloomy as if the Jinn were already at work all around heaven in disguise. Quietly I landed on the balcony of God's home. Pushing the curtain to the side, I looked to the left. Looking down the stairs, I saw a shadow in the room to the right. I slowly made my way down the stairs and flicked my wrist.

"Nathaniel," a soft female voice said through the darkness from behind me.

When I looked, I saw nothing. I wondered if what I heard was just in my head. There was something sinister at work here; I could feel it. Suddenly two swords crashed together. I looked back in the direction I had been walking. It was what appeared to be a Jinn fighting a female human. The human wielded a katana that was unfamiliar to me. Her fighting style was identical to my own. I knew she saved my life, but for what reason? Suddenly, another Jinn came from out of nowhere and tried to hit her, but this was no ordinary female human. She engaged both of her opponents with much skill and was well versed in Ranin Mana. When I saw God walk into the chaos, I knew it was over, and a sigh of relief came over me. But I was wrong. This was not God. When he walked up to me, I did not fear him. I should have, though. Suddenly, a sword appeared in his hands, and he drove its blade straight through my chest. It was only then that I knew that this was not God but just a nasty shape-shifting Jinn. It was too late, though. I fell to my knees. I had blood all over my hands. My sword disappeared. My limp body fell to the floor. I felt the life leaving my body as I continued to watch this human kill Jinn. Then she walked over to me putting her katana in the sheath that she had on her back.

"Nathaniel? Can you hear me?" she said. "Tigist, I need you."

When I heard her call Tigist, it was then that I knew this was no mere human being. It was Enreal. With everything still fading, I saw an owl fly over and perch itself on the girl's shoulder. Whispering something to the owl, she gently put her hands over my wound. Feeling much pressure, I watched as she slowly pulled her hand away from my chest. Unable to keep my eyes open, they shut. I felt as if I died, seeing bright flickering lights all over. Then suddenly, everything came into focus. I saw our Inauguration Day. I remember Inauguration Day very well. I thought to myself, *Could it be that I've died and these are just memories coming to me from in my unconscious mind?* I was being shown the first day I fell deeply in love with Maya. I remember how beautiful she was that day. Her smile, the way the sun hit her brown hair, she was a sight to see. Waking up in a cold sweat, I sat up and looked around. I was at home in my bed. *How did I get here?* I thought. Rubbing my head, I looked at the bedroom door, and in walked Maya.

"Maya," I said, happy to see her.

"Nathaniel, are you okay?" Maya said as I gave her a tight hug.

"Where's the girl?" I asked, confused.

"What girl?" Maya asked, confused.

"How did I get home?"

"You're acting really weird. Are you okay?"

"I'm not sure."

"What's wrong, Nathaniel?"

"I don't know."

"We have to get dressed now. Something isn't right."

Without asking any more questions, Maya and I got our armors on and quickly flew off into the sky. Calling on the elders one at a time till we were all together, we flew to the home of God.

"Nathaniel, would you mind telling me what we are doing at my father's home?" Everin asked.

"Were under attack."

"My children, why have you come?" It was God.

"Father, Nathaniel believes that we are under attack by the Jinn and we don't even know it."

"Nathaniel, why do you say these things?"

"Because it is true," I said as I flicked my wrist and drove my katana through God's chest as I grabbed him on the back of the neck and ground my teeth, throwing him to the ground. All the elders flicked their wrists, but Maya.

"Nathaniel! What've you done?" Everin asked.

"No, Everin, your father has been taken or slain. This thing is just a Jinn mimicking your father."

"You will all burn in its fire. You will all die. The dark one has risen," the Jinn mimicking God said in an evil voice.

Suddenly, the sky became dark, and it began to rain violently. Thunder and lightning came crashing down, hitting God's home and splitting it in two. As I looked at the sky, I saw the Jinn everywhere. It looked like a terrible nightmare. Evil and darkness were everywhere now. Without command, I flew off into the sky and engaged the Jinn. The fellowship of the elders was now broken, and I knew someone had betrayed us.

"Everin, we must help Nathaniel," said Maya.

"He's made his choice. He stands alone now."

"Everin, your father would have never allowed Nathaniel to disband from us."

"I'm sorry, Maya. Nathaniel is lost to us now."

"Lucifer?"

"Sorry, Maya. I can't go against the princess," said Lucifer.

***

Maya

My eyes filled with tears as I watched the elders flying to the sky in the opposite direction of Nathaniel. As a group, they engaged the Jinn. Reaching a fork in the road, I had to make my choice. *Do I follow my heart with Nathaniel, or do I follow orders?* Just then, a Jinn six feet tall stood before me. In his hand was a bloodied battle ax. As he swung it at me, I swiftly dodged his febrile attacks. When finally it came down and hit my katana holding him steady for just a moment, I punched him as hard as I could in the stomach. As he fell back, a sword from behind him went straight through his body. It was Everin.

"Maya, I'm sorry. Let's help Nathaniel," Everin said to me.

As Everin and I began to fly off to help Nathaniel, a swarm of Jinn came from out of nowhere and scooped Everin up and disappeared into the darkness of the sky.

"Everin, no!" I yelled, watching as she was carried away.

I continued flying toward Nathaniel to help him, and I saw that the elders all stood next to him once more. To my eyes, the fellowship of the elders had been restored. It was then that the sky lightened up again as the Jinn retreated and returned to whence they came.

"Nathaniel, they took her," I said, weeping as the elders looked on me in sadness.

"Maya, we'll get her back. Can you fly?" Nathaniel asked, gently placing his hand on my shoulder and giving me a hug.

"Yes."

"Let's regroup. Let's fly."

Paradise Lost

Dark times fell over heaven with the disappearance of the royal family. The elders heard of the dark one who rose from the ashes of the abyss to create the Jinn. One by one, the realms fell to the Jinn and turned into cesspools of evil and hate. What was once known as the abyss now became known as hell. Hell in the angelic script meant "evil."

"Roquin, Everin, Eden, and God. Why have we been spared? Roquin was my friend. He was the best of us, and Everin, she was the love of my life," Lucifer said, upset.

"If they're just taking them, we must ask ourselves what is being done with them. That would also mean that they're still alive," Maya said, thinking.

"There's nothing that suggests to me that we have been spared. We're broken. It's only a matter of time before the Jinn make their final attack. Then we'll all be finished," Nathaniel said sadly.

"Nathaniel, what of Everin?" Lucifer asked. "The two of you were always more than just friends."

"What are you insinuating?" Nathaniel asked, getting angry.

"Nothing," Lucifer said as if he knew something no one else did.

"Elders, we need to evacuate heaven. We need to bestow upon all human citizens who are willing the blessing of reincarnation. It is the only way to save them. We should put together a small militia of every able-bodied angel to make one last attempt to save those we've lost."

"What you're talking about is suicide," Maya said, concerned.

"Nathaniel, I'm in," Lucifer said.

"What am I going to do with you?" Maya said, looking at Nathaniel, shaking her head. "I'm in."

"Okay, I will go to my realm and do what I can to form a militia to go into hell to rescue the souls we can. But this thing could go sour quickly, and if that happens, don't be careless with your lives. Descend to earth."

"Nathaniel, there's only one problem with that. How do we descend without God's permission? No one has ever done it, and the consequences for doing so could be severe."

"It's a risk we're going to have to take. I will see to the militia. Maya, Lucifer, you two go now and see to the reincarnation of as many humans as possible."

Nathaniel went to the angels of his realm and asked those who were willing to join him and help in the evacuation of heaven.

"These have become dark times, my friends. Through the decades, I have become close to many of you, and to some, I am known to you as your champion. But in this time of chaos, it's no longer you that calls on I. Rise up with me. Help me now to save as many of us as we can," Nathaniel said to the citizens of his realm.

"Nathaniel, your words fall on deaf ears," Rylin said, laughing.

"That's enough from you!" an angel shouted, punching Rylin to the ground. "Nathaniel, you are our champion, and we answer the call."

"How dare you put your hands on me. Do you know who I am?" Rylin said, angry.

"Oh, Rylin, you would think you'd have learned by now. There's only one voice that matters here, and it is definitely not yours."

"But . . ."

"But nothing, Rylin. You should join us in the fight now. Remember all the arguments Everin went through defending you. Will you not join us now to possibly save her?"

"Nathaniel, you and I have never seen eye to eye nor ever bothered to. Perhaps we can begin here and now," Rylin said as he put his hand out to shake Nathaniel's.

"Together we will all stand. Never fearing, never forgetting, and never forgiving," Nathaniel said to all the citizens of the realm, and they cheered. "Gather any weapons you can to fight the Jinn. Our war begins now. This is where they meet their end. We'll raid hell together and end this once and for all."

When Nathaniel returned to Maya and Lucifer, he was met with great news of the number of citizens they reincarnated, but he knew he had to return to his realm to join the militia he had begun.

"I must leave you once more, Maya, to lead the militia into hell. You and Lucifer need to stay and liberate more of our citizens."

"Nathaniel, let me come with you," Lucifer asked.

"You cannot. You must stay," I told Lucifer. "I must leave now."

"Nathaniel, please return to me."

"Intact, my love. I promise," Nathaniel said as he kissed her on the lips.

That night, Maya had a nightmare that Nathaniel was killed by a horde of Jinn. Fearing the death of her loved one, she prayed to God.

"Dear Lord, I pray that wherever you may be, you are safe and well. I'm not sure if you can hear me, but Nathaniel is coming to find you and the others. He has not given up hope that you're still out there. I ask that you keep him steadfast and with a ready sword. Things have not been the same since your absence. With the grace you have shown me, I will continue to stand firm and have faith in Nathaniel's word. Amen."

The next morning, Maya awoke with a splitting headache. Something in her mind was telling her that Nathaniel was in trouble. Grabbing her armor, she flew out the door. A heavy cloud cover began to form like always before accompanied by Jinn. Once more, the thunder and lightning struck. In the distance, she could see Lucifer.

"Lucifer, where are you going?" Maya asked, flying up next to him.

"Nathaniel needs us. I can feel it," Lucifer responded.

As they looked ahead, they could see God's home. Nathaniel's militia stood outside. Lucifer and Maya picked up speed to get to Nathaniel quicker. As the water from the rain began dripping off her armor, she flicked her wrist and Lucifer and Maya came down from the sky and stood next to Nathaniel.

"Maya, Lucifer, there is something wrong," Nathaniel said worriedly.

"What is it, Nathaniel?" Lucifer asked.

"I don't know. It's something I've never felt before, something elusive, something dreadfully evil," Nathaniel said concerned. "We're being watched." The three of them and the militia looked up at the balcony of God's home.

Coming from out of the shadows, a dark entity appeared, holding an angel by the back of the neck.

"Nathaniel, don't believe its lies! Escape this place!" the angel shouted.

"You shut your mouth," the dark entity said, punching the angel in the side.

"Nathaniel, it's Eden," Maya said.

"Listen to me, elders. Lay down your katanas and surrender, or you will meet the same fate as your friends," the dark entity shouted.

"Nathaniel, what should we do?" Lucifer asked, concerned.

"You dare threaten her life?" Nathaniel shouted at the entity.

"Oh, I dare," it said in a dark, eerie voice. "Now surrender."

"Nathaniel, you mustn't!" Eden shouted.

"This conversation is over. Kill them all!"

Before the elders could say or do anything, the dark entity slit Eden's throat, and as she bled out, her once white robe became red, and her lifeless body was dropped from the balcony. Hordes of Jinn came flying toward them. The militia stood tall and brave, but it soon broke, and the elders and Rylin were the only ones left.

"Rylin!" Lucifer yelled as Rylin fled cowardly. "I always knew he was a coward," Lucifer said before becoming overwhelmed by Jinn.

"Maya, I have to get into the house," Nathaniel said.

"Nathaniel, it's suicide. We must descend to earth. Heaven is lost. Why are you doing this?"

"I don't know why. There's a voice in my head that's telling me Everin is still alive. I can feel it," Nathaniel calmly said through all the chaos around them. "I have to do this."

"Nathaniel, is there anything about Everin I should know?"

"No."

"Then I'll go with you."

"No, you must survive this, Maya," Nathaniel said, looking at her beautiful face. "You must."

"You don't make sense, Nathaniel. Please, come with me," Maya said, sternly grinding her teeth. "Heaven's lost. You and I are all that remains. Roquin, Everin, Eden, God, now Lucifer. I won't lose you too!"

"I love you, Maya. I'll find you on earth," Nathaniel said, looking deep into Maya's eyes. "Now descend to earth. That's an order," Nathaniel said, turning his back and walking toward the house, killing every foe that came at him.

"Nathaniel, I love you."

Maya took off flying into the sky like a rocket. When she felt she was high enough, she came soaring back down through the dark clouds and rain, ripping through any Jinn in her path. An angel had never flown as fast as Maya did that day, breaking the sound barrier. She broke through heaven's crust, and suddenly from another direction, something that appeared to be an angel slammed into the side of God's home. Nathaniel made his way through the Jinn when he came across Lucifer.

"Nathaniel, where are you going?" Lucifer said, still fighting Jinn with every breath he had.

"I must get in God's home."

"I understand, my friend. Let me clear a path for you," Lucifer said, picking up one of the bloodied swords from the ground.

"Lucifer."

"I'm spent, Nathaniel," Lucifer said, spitting up blood. "Besides, all my family is here, and I can't imagine a more glorious death than helping my brother." He took a deep breath. "Now out of my way, old friend," Lucifer said, smiling.

Lucifer, using all the Ranin Mana inside him, flew through the Jinn in Nathaniel's path, mowing them down and obliterating their very existence, till he finally succumbed to his injuries and disappeared into a horde of Jinn. Nathaniel continued fighting any leftover Jinn in his path. When he walked through the entryway door of God's home, he saw Everin's nude body sprawled out in the middle of the entryway in a ritualistic manner. Her face was swollen and pummeled to the point of being unrecognizable. Her body had been so violated. There were bite marks all over her chest, and the nipple of her left breast had been torn. Holding back his tears, Nathaniel walked over to her and gently placed his hand on her forehead. On the floor next to her, he saw the Elder Grimoire.

"Nathaniel," Everin said in a shallow voice.

"Oh my God, Everin, don't talk."

"It's too late for me, Nathaniel. You must save the twins."

"Twins?"

"Nathaniel, you must know," Everin said, gasping for air. "I must tell you, the twins are . . . are—" Everin stuttered and gasped before passing away.

"Everin, Everin! No, God, please," Nathaniel said, crying.

Just then, Nathaniel heard what sounded like two infant children crying. He stood up, and in the doorway of one of the rooms stood the dark entity once more. In its arms, he saw a child. The entity then vanished, and Nathaniel heard another cry from an infant. He grabbed the Elder Grimoire.

When Nathaniel walked into the room where the dark entity had been standing in the doorway, he saw a woman dressed in black, holding another child and fighting Jinn at the same time. As he quickly ran to help her, he noticed it was Enreal.

"Nathaniel!" she said as they both fought the Jinn. "I need you to take this child and descend to earth. You will be safe there. The cross around his neck must stay on him at all times. It will keep him hidden from our enemies trying to find him.

"I can't leave you here like this, Enreal! I can't leave Everin."

"You need to! Now go. I will hold them here! Heaven has fallen, Nathaniel! Go!"

Against his will, Nathaniel did as Enreal instructed. As soon as he took the baby from Enreal, more Jinn than he had ever seen before began attacking as he flew through the air. They were after the child. He burst through the ceiling of God's home, sheltering the baby from the debris and any Jinn that stood in his path. He looked back and saw Enreal disappear into the darkness. Like

Maya had done before him, when he reached a suitable height, he turned and flew as fast he could toward heaven's crust. Breaking the sound barrier, he flew through all the Jinn in his path. He hit the crust, and as he broke through it, he began to feel pain all over his wings as if they were being burned off his back. He held the baby tight, and as the pain began to become unbearable, everything went dark.

New World

Nathaniel

Feeling cold water hit my face, I opened my eyes. I could taste saltwater and sand. Picking my head up, I began to look around. Darkness was everywhere. The only light was that of the moon. The pain of my wings was gone. As I stood up, I noticed that I was nude and my once beautiful wings were gone now. I looked farther up the coast of the beach and saw a campfire. I heard a baby cry. Struggling to walk, my legs felt like dead weight. With every step I took, I could feel the cold wet sand under my feet. When I came closer to the campfire, I could hear there was more than one baby—three to be exact. One was crying while the other two were cooing at each other.

"Brice, can you grab Connor? I think his diaper needs to be changed," a sweet female voice said.

"Sure, honey," a male voice responded. "Come here, big guy," Brice said, picking up a baby from a playpen.

"You're super cute, aren't you?" the female said, cooing over the baby she was holding. "Isn't he a cutie, Octavia?" she said to the other baby lying on a beach towel.

It was then I knew she was holding Everin's baby. I watched this family embrace him with love as if he were their own. For a moment, I thought about just leaving him with them, thinking this would keep him hidden and safe from whoever might be looking for him. What did I know of babies? What would I teach him in years to come? But my heart told me this would be wrong.

I was entrusted with his life, to keep him safe. Grabbing one of their beach towels, I wrapped it around myself.

"How are you doing tonight?" I asked as I walked up to the couple casually.

"We're fine. Were you swimming in the ocean, sir?" The female smiled and asked as if she knew me somehow.

"I was. I see you met my son."

"He's very cute, sir. What's his name?" she asked, picking up Octavia.

"His name?" I asked, surprised.

"Yes, what's this little cutie's name?" she said as she snuggled both the babies.

"Um, Jensen. Jensen Kane. I'm Nathaniel Kane, and that's Kane with a *K*," I said, smiling. Unbeknownst to them that I took the first name from their stroller brand and the last name from a walking cane hanging from the handlebar.

"Kane with a *K*, ah," she said, nodding and smirking. "I'm Alyssa, and this is my husband, Brice. These are our twins, Connor and Octavia."

"Octavia, that's a beautiful name."

"Thank you. You'd laugh if you knew how I came up with it."

"How'd you come up with it?"

"I named her after the word *octaves*, which are the interval between two notes in vocal pitch. I'm quite the music fanatic." Alyssa laughed. "But I guess it goes with the territory."

"How's that?"

"I'm the owner of Nuclear Bullet Records," Alyssa said as she smiled. "Listen, we're just about to start eating some dinner coming off the BBQ. Would you and Jensen like to join us?"

"No, thank you, we really need to be going."

"I understand."

As Alyssa stood up, I could see that the cane on the stroller belonged to her because her foot was in a brace. When I took Jensen from her, he began to make adorable cooing noises. Once I held him and looked into his eyes, a feeling of unconditional love came over me. This was something I hadn't felt in a long time. I thought this must've been how God felt the first time he held Everin. In that moment, I fell in love and knew that this was what

I had been created for. This was my destiny—to love him, guide him, and die for him if need be. I gave myself to him completely. I was now his father. Octavia and Connor both began making cute cooing noises. It was as if they were speaking to Jensen in their own special way.

"Alyssa, you're not going to just let this guy take the baby. We don't even know if he's telling us the truth," Brice said, getting mad.

"Brice, we are going to let him take the baby. Jensen belongs with him. Nathaniel is his father. Now go Nathaniel, and may God be with you," Alyssa said, gently stroking her fingers on Jensen's cheek. "I know who you are, Jensen Kane. I will see you again soon," Alyssa said as she softly kissed Jensen on the cheek. "Nathaniel, at the top of the hill, you will find a parking lot. Look for the emerald-green Chevy Silverado. The door will be unlocked. Open the envelope on the front seat."

"Who are you, Alyssa?" I asked suspiciously.

"You will know in all good time. Enreal had planned for your arrival from heaven."

"Alyssa! Are we really going to help this guy? We don't even know for sure if it's him."

"My love, you need to trust my judgment," Alyssa said, softly placing her hand on his chest.

"All right, go in peace, Nathaniel," Brice said, nodding yes.

How did she know Enreal? I thought as I walked barefoot through the cold sand.

I felt the sand move up between my toes with every step. As I came to a very steep hill, I climbed it and saw three people walking toward me. Feeling paranoid, I moved out of their way, holding Jensen tight, ready to flick my wrist at the slightest gesture of evil. When I reached the top, there was a parking lot just as Alyssa said. I looked for the Chevy Silverado. Finding it, I walked on the hard pavement. Checking the door, I pulled up on the handle, and it was unlocked. I got in. Lying Jensen on the passenger seat, I noticed the envelope Alyssa spoke of.

Dear Nathaniel,

I know it must've been hard for you to leave me fighting those Jinn in hell, but I assure you, I'm alive and well. Jensen is your warrant for walking the earth, Nathaniel. Every step you've ever taken has been leading to this. Jensen is your son, your reason for living. He'll need your guidance and look for it often. He will stumble and fall, but in time, he will mold into the angel that will help shape and change the world.

Believe me when I tell you the worst is still yet to come. He carries the sigil of Spraygin, the pitchfork underneath his right arm. It's his birthright. The Nevillin prophesied his birth, as it also prophesied mine. The wooden cross I put around his neck should never be removed, for it shields him from evil. The wood is that of a large splinter taken from the cross of Christ.

I have made all the proper arrangements with my grandmother for your arrival. You must document the fall of heaven into the Elder Grimoire. You must be specific in your account of this tragedy. I swear through all that has been lost, there is a light at the end of the tunnel. The truck is a gift along with the keys to a home. The cell phone has only one number in it, which belongs to my grandmother, Alyssa Kryst. As soon as you turn the phone on, it will tell you how to get to your home. I have also taken the liberty of setting up a place of employment for you. You are going to be working for Alyssa at her company, Nuclear Bullet Records. She will teach you everything you will need to know about the business. You need to raise Jensen as human as possible. This will also help in keeping him hidden. There will be a time someday when he will no longer have to stay in hiding, and he will seek out all that is evil and try to bring an end to the terror."

PS. Thought you would like to know that when you get to the home, there is someone already there that can't wait to see you. If you need anything, please do not hesitate to call my grandmother. She will see that all your needs are met. You are my family, Nathaniel, and I love you more than you know.

Enreal

Putting the key into the ignition, I started the truck. I put my hand on the side of Jensen's face. I told him I loved him as I put the truck in reverse. When I drove up to the house, it had a pine tree in front close to an entry gate. The house was brown with a three-car garage. I pushed the button on the visor, and the garage opened. To my surprise as the garage raised up, there in the doorway of the house stood the love of my life, Maya. I pulled into the garage, grabbed Jensen. I couldn't get out fast enough.

"Nathaniel," Maya said, smiling, embracing me with a hug and kiss.

"I was so worried about you. How did you find this place?" I asked as we held each other.

"Enreal. She saved me," Maya said, looking at Jensen. "Who's this little one?"

"That's a long story. We have much to discuss."

***

As the years passed, my friendship with Alyssa became strong. Through Alyssa, Maya and I learned that she is a descendant of Jesus Christ. Through the generations, the name of Christ was in danger because Jinn were trying to kill the bloodline. So the Christ family adopted and slightly changed the spelling of the name to stay hidden. Where it was once spelled *C-h-r-i-s-t*, it transformed and became spelled *K-r-y-s-t*.

I became very well known in the music industry and gained Nuclear Bullet Records many new musical talents. It gave me a sense of pride and made me feel good when I was being sought out by many different prestigious record labels. I became so busy that I brought in Maya to be my assistant in the business, and we became very accustomed to many of the beautiful blessings of human life. We were now known as the Kane family, never forgetting who we were or where we came from. We vowed to raise Jensen to be a hard-working, respectful person, growing up alongside Alyssa's children. The three of them became inseparable. From birthdays, holidays, to surfing on the beach, they were always together.

It was when Jensen turned twelve that we began seeing a decrease in his grades, and a violent temper emerged. His school began counseling him and talking to us about possibly expelling him after he lashed out at a teacher, scaring those around him at times with his violent outbursts. There were only a few people that could talk to him and cool his temper—at home, Maya and I. At school, Octavia kept a close eye on him. It was then that I decided he would be trained in mixed martial arts, and he also had to be trained in how to properly use the Ranin Mana that ran through his blood. I hoped that the discipline of mixed martial arts would ease his temper and humble his spirit. I also extended the invitation to Octavia and Connor. The training was to begin immediately.

The Nevillin

Nathaniel

As the kids sat on the grass in the backyard and looked at me with their big eyes so eager to hear what I was going to say next, I started, "Now listen, all of you. I have trained a militia before. I've even trained and versed myself well in mixed martial arts. But I've never taught kids before. I can tell you that this is not going to be easy, but it will teach you discipline and assist in molding your spirit, mind, and body. When I feel you are ready, I will teach you to fight with melee weapons, and then I will teach you how to properly combine the two. Octavia is a girl, but you boys don't for one minute underestimate what she is capable of. Where I come from, our women were revered as the bravest of warriors. Now let's begin. We will start with you, Connor."

"Me, sir?" Connor said, surprised.

"Is your name Connor?" I smiled.

"Yes."

"Then stand up. Show me a fighting stance . . . or what you think a fighting stance should look like," Nathaniel said looking at Connor as he formed a stance. "I see you watch those kung-fu movies. Bruce Lee, Jet Lee, Chuck Norris, Van Damme—all of them are very good fighters. Now combine them together, and what do you have?"

"I'm not sure." Connor shrugged.

"A really good fighter," Octavia answered when she was called on after raising her hand.

"The perfect fighting engine," Jensen responded after he was called on.

"A really good fighter, the perfect fighting engine. Both very excellent answers," I said, pointing at each of them as I repeated their answers. "How about sublimity? They only became as great as they did because they applied themselves and never gave up. The discipline that they learned through martial arts is what guided them. But what you all are going to learn will be far more useful. You are going to learn mixed martial arts from Jeet Kune Do, tae kwon do, Brazilian jiujitsu, aikido, and Keysi fighting method for close combat fighting. When you master these techniques, you will learn kendo, which is using martial arts practices and values and applying them to swordsmanship. When you have mastered all these, you will become a force to be reckoned with."

***

Jensen

As days turned to weeks and weeks turned to months, mixed martial arts became a way of life. I could feel my soul becoming one with my body. I learned to harness Ranin Mana and use it only to my advantage when need be. I began learning and understanding things faster. We were sponges, and all of us absorbed Nathaniel's teachings and philosophy. He would often tell us stories of heaven and what it was like to be an elder angel.

When we learned kendo, it was my mother that taught us. We all thought that learning under Nathaniel was hard. When my mother taught, it was like an endurance trial. We could not fall behind, and she would not repeat herself ever. Thank God when she started teaching us kendo, we began with wooden sticks.

"Octavia, Jensen, team up. You will be sparring against Connor and I," Maya said, walking out of the house and into the grass. "We're not using those today," she added as we began getting the wooden sticks.

"What are we going to be using?"

"These," Maya said as she set down a black bag with two swords in it.

"There are only two swords in here," Octavia said as she looked in the bag.

"Jensen, come here," Nathaniel said as he walked out onto the patio. "Do you remember the stories I told you about your mother?"

"Yes," I replied.

"Do you remember the stories I told you about the katana she wielded?"

"The Nevillin," I replied.

"Her katana was part of her bloodline. She may have died, but her bloodline did not," Nathaniel said, looking deep into my eyes. "Her spirit lives inside you, son. The Nevillin belongs to you because you will use it for good. It has always been drawn to the light. Her katana was an extension of her. The Nevillin now resides within you."

"That means . . ."

"Yes, go on and flick your wrist for the first time. When you do this, you are calling on the Nevillin. The Nevillin is not just any katana. It is the katana that prophesied your birth," Nathaniel said as I flicked my wrist and the Nevillin appeared.

"It's beautiful," I said, touching the blade.

"It's your birthright, Jensen," Nathaniel said.

"What sigil is this, Dad?" I asked, looking at the sigil on the blade.

"Well, that's new," Nathaniel said, looking at the sigil that appeared above my own. "Maya, come take a look at this."

"Well, that's new," Maya said, looking at the blade.

"That's what I said."

As the three of us stood and looked at the blade of the Nevillin, Octavia and Connor walked over and looked on too. We watched as angelic sigils began to appear all over the blade of the Nevillin. It would come slowly in the light-blue glow and then brand the sigil into the blade.

"Lucifer, Roquin, Nathaniel, Maya, Eden, Godric Goodwater," Nathaniel said aloud.

"Godric Goodwater, who's Godric Goodwater?" Maya asked, confused.

"Dad, there's more on the other side, but they don't look like sigils," I said, continuing to hold the Nevillin.

"Combine the fallen," Nathaniel said aloud.

"What does that mean?" Maya asked, confused.

"I'm not sure," Nathaniel said, unconvincing.

"Why don't we just get back to training for now? Jensen, show us what you've learned," Nathaniel said as we all walked onto the grass.

"Nathaniel," Maya said sternly.

"Maya, now's not the time," Nathaniel said under his breath.

"I understand, but don't be thinking we're not going to be having this conversation later."

"Understood."

"Light combat, guys. We're not trying to kill one another. But if for some reason you are hurt, you go see Nathaniel. When going in for a hit, you are to stop before you make contact and tap them on the shoulder," Maya said firmly, looking at us. "Connor, you're with me."

Gathering myself, I grasped the Nevillin tight. Looking at the angelic sigils, I couldn't help but wonder who this Godric Goodwater character must be. When Maya said, "Fight!" I came at her swinging as I saw Octavia fight Connor. Her strokes were perfect until Maya began working me over close to where they were fighting. Maya suddenly blocked one of my attacks and threw me to the ground. She quickly along with Connor began attacking Octavia till she hit Connor's sword out of the way and tapped Octavia on the forearm. Turning to my skills in the Keysi fighting method, I engaged them both. Then something unusual happened. It was unlike anything I'd felt before. I began moving so fast that everything stood still. I was able to tap Connor on the side of his waist without drawing blood. Coming back at my mother, she blocked every swing I made at her. Until suddenly Nathaniel jumped in and began helping my mother defeat me. Even when I would move fast and slow everything down, I still could not hit either one of them. Till what I thought was luck, I cut my mother on the upper left arm.

"You're on your own, Nathaniel," Maya said, walking off the grass.

Running at Nathaniel with everything I had, I became that force to be reckoned with. Nathaniel then caught one of the many punches I threw at him. Holding me there, he went to tap me on the side of my waist when I reversed the hold he had me in and came in an upward motion with the Nevillin. In slow motion, I glided across his chest without cutting him.

"You have much heart and determination, Jensen. What you learned was how to use and combine all your skills with Ranin Mana. Ranin Mana was the gift God gave the elder angels," Nathaniel said, looking at me. "The mana that flows through you was passed to you genetically by your mother."

"You all did marvelous. You all surpassed what I thought you were capable of," Maya said, smiling.

"I'm sorry I cut you, Mom," I said, walking over to her.

"Jensen, there is nothing to be sorry for. I'm so proud of you."

"What is the sigil on the Nevillin here near the handle?" I asked, pointing at it.

"The angelic sigil here is the sigil that's on your arm," Nathaniel said as he pointed to one of the two sigils. "Spraygin, this is your sigil. It appeared on the Nevillin when it was created. Translated in angelic script, it means 'the guardian.' This one on the opposite side, the sigil is Enreal. Angelic script translates to 'the savior.'"

"Who's Enreal?" I asked.

"I'm not sure," Nathaniel said, looking as if he knew but didn't want to say.

"Who created angelic scripture?" Octavia asked.

"You kids have the greatest questions." Nathaniel chuckled. "I created the scripture. Its alphabet focuses on signs, sigils."

"Does Mom know that you created it?" Jensen said, shocked.

"I can't hide anything from your mother," Nathaniel said, smiling at Maya as she smiled back.

Godric Goodwater

Nathaniel

Maya asked as the kids jumped on their bikes and left. "Nathaniel, are you ready to talk now? Who is Godric Goodwater? And I don't want to hear that you don't know."

"We should sit down. There's much I need to tell you," I said as we took a seat in the backyard.

"Godric Goodwater," I said, taking a deep breath and exhaling. "Godric Goodwater is the true name of God," I said, looking at Maya.

"How is it that you know this?"

"A possessed young boy in hell told me before God became one with his katana."

"What do you mean 'became one with his katana'? God never had a katana."

"He did. It's called the Nexus. Our katanas are extensions of ourselves. They are our fail-safe and assurance that our spirits will never be lost. We are bound to our katana as God was to his," I said as I flicked my wrist and the Nexus appeared.

"This was God's? The design on the handle is beautiful, and the angelic script down both sides of the blade is amazing."

"Yes, it is. Eden had a katana as well. I've never seen it, but I'm sure it was equally as beautiful."

"Eden had a katana? I feel like I'm discovering things I should've already known."

"Don't feel like that."

"It's as if he created our katanas and made them the source of our powers purposely."

"I believe he did."

"But why?"

"I believe he had foreseen his demise. Maybe he didn't know how it would happen, but he knew it would, and therefore, he wanted something of himself to remain. In foreseeing his own demise, he granted us, his elders, the same blessing. "

"What does the script say?" Maya asked.

"The script reveals God's true name and his origin. It speaks of combining the fallen katanas."

"You mean it reveals how he came to be? What does it mean, combine the fallen katanas?" Maya asked. "Did you read about his origin?"

"I'm unable to read the scripture that it's written in; it's a writing that I'm unfamiliar with."

"Enreal, has read it?"

"I believe the Nexus is the katana she wields."

"When you said the boy in the hell was possessed, what did you mean?"

"*Possessed* was the term God used to refer to those who had a Jinn inside them, whispering to them, guiding them to do evil deeds and commit horrible acts."

"Why were the elders never made aware of possessions?"

"God and I made a pact to never tell anyone of what we were doing till we knew what we were dealing with."

"How did the human beings in the hell become possessed?"

"We never knew. I believe the dark one who rose to create the Jinn had something to do with it. The boy was possessed by a Jinn that referred to itself as Zeyreal. Let me tell you what happened."

It was dark, windy, and raining in the hell. The sadness there was overwhelming. I saw buildings that were falling apart and humans of earth sitting in the wreckage. They were in deep and infinite sadness. It was as if this place wasn't even hell anymore, but something else. There were no angels anywhere. God had told me that the deeper we journeyed, the sadder it would become, and that if you're not careful, the sadness would overcome your mind and you would become stuck there.

God and I had our katanas drawn, and we were ready for anything. As we walked, he told me how proud he was of me. He also told me that if anything were to ever happen to him that I was to guide Everin through any trials and tribulations she might face. When we found the boy, he was curled up in the corner of an abandoned building.

"Heaven falling will be the last thing you ever see, old sage," the boy said in a sinister eerie voice, looking up at God.

"Boy, reveal to us your name."

"The boy no longer resides here, Godric."

"What did you call me?"

"Godric, that is your name, isn't it?" the boy said with an eerie laugh. "I'm Zeyreal."

"Where'd you hear that name?"

"The dark one and I have so much fun I've been told many things. Why do you look scared?" The boy laughed. "Perhaps there's something you wish for me not to say aloud? "

"Nathaniel, take the Nexus," God said, looking at me.

"My Lord?"

"Take it, Nathaniel, and start walking back the way we came. Everything will be fine. Zeyreal is mine."

"As you wish," I said, reluctant to listen as Zeyreal sinisterly smiled.

"So now that he has parted, what should we talk about, Godric?" Zeyreal said, smiling and mocking. "You never told them, did you? Your real name. The sage you once were."

"I'll make you a deal. Let me grant that boy your possessing reincarnation," God said, looking Zeyreal in the eye. "If you allow this, I'll submit."

"No! Let him take me, Lord," I said, coming out from the shadows.

"Nathaniel, I told you to go back."

"Doesn't listen very well, does he?" Zeyreal said, looking at me.

"Nathaniel, this is not your time. You must leave this place."

"I will not. I won't leave you here with this thing."

"You will, Nathaniel. Now release the boy, Zeyreal. I'll give him to Nathaniel. You allow them to go peacefully, and I'm yours."

Before my eyes, I watched as Zeyreal released the boy from his grasp like smoke coming from a pipe. Zeyreal then looked at

God. Taking the boy by the arm, God pulled him slowly toward himself.

"Nathaniel, take the boy and leave this place."

"I don't remember agreeing to anything about saying goodbyes, Godric," Zeyreal said with an eerie laugh. "Godric, Koric, Athena. No doubt the sons and daughter of Oric Goodwater. Left on your own to create humans, what a waste. All to save Arthonia. Sages they shall forever be, eternal are the three . . ."

In mid-sentence, I leaped over God with the Nexus in my hand. I swung at Zeyreal, hitting him. He let out a ghastly roar before disappearing into thin air. Looking behind me, I saw the boy, but God vanished slowly till nothing remained but a faint blue light, no doubt his soul. The blue light entered the Nexus, and a sigil unknown to me appeared. Taking the boy by the hand, I flew us both from hell to safety and bestowed upon the boy reincarnation.

"I can't believe he's gone," Maya said.

"Physically maybe, but I don't believe we've seen the last of him."

"You should have told me all this long ago," Maya said disappointed. "Did Everin know?"

"I don't know."

"Who were Oric, Koric, and Athena?"

"I have no idea."

"Is there anything else I should know?" Maya asked as if she knew something else was lingering in my mind. "Any other secrets?"

"No I believe Godric's soul now rests within the Nexus."

"I'm unfamiliar with these entities that Zeyreal spoke of," I said. "Whoever they are, I'm sure we'll find out one day."

The Deal

Jensen

The warmth of the sun was beautiful as I sat up on my surfboard and let it beat down on me. I took a deep breath and exhaled with my eyes shut. I thought, *What could be better than this?* My feet were dangling in the water. I could feel the coolness of the water move in between my toes. I looked at Octavia sitting there on her board in a bikini that revealed every perfect curve of her body, thinking, *She is so beautiful.* The water dripped down her skin and the rays of the sun made her glisten. I don't know why, but if ever in my life I didn't believe in God, I could look at her and know he exists. Looking back at the shore, I saw Connor with my parents coming down the hill that entered the beach.

"I'm going to marry you," I said, looking at Octavia.

"What makes you so sure, Jensen Kane?" Octavia replied.

"I know things. I'm confident we will be married one day."

"Are you proposing, Jensen Kane?" Octavia said, smiling.

"No, I'm only seventeen. I'm too young. But I promise, when the time comes, I'll put a ring on your finger."

"I guess we'll just have to wait and see then," Octavia said, lying down on her board and paddling away.

"I guess so." I smirked.

"Jensen, you have so much to learn about yourself before you ever truly will understand the opposite sex," Maya said, paddling over next to me.

"I love her, Mom. I know I'm young and have much to learn, but the one thing I know is there's nothing I wouldn't do for her."

"I understand. You are so much like your father."

"How long have you and Dad been together?"

"I've known your father my whole life since we were kids. We grew up arguing most of the time, no different really than now. But for all the years I've known your father, he has always been a very complicated angel, but if one thing is true about that man, it's that he always puts his family first, and he loves us with all his heart," Maya said, looking at me. "Even after heaven was lost and your mother passed away, Nathaniel still never gave up hope on humanity or us."

"How did heaven fall?"

"The elders and God were betrayed by one of our own. We never found out by whom, but I believe that being is still alive because the Jinn are still out there," Maya said, saddened by what she was telling me. "Before heaven fell, God went missing."

"I know he became one with his katana."

"Where'd you hear that?" Maya said, shocked.

"I heard you and Dad talking. I know of the boy in hell and his possession."

"You know, even though Nathaniel may not be your real father, you have so much of him in you, especially that rebel side of him. Don't ever lose that."

"What are you guys talking about?" Nathaniel asked, swimming up on his board with Connor following.

Suddenly, we heard the most terrifying scream. It sounded like Octavia. As my mother, father, and I looked over in the direction the scream came from, we saw Octavia's board floating in the water. In an instant, she came up out of the water, gasping for air and quickly being pulled under the water again. I quickly lied down on my board and swam over to where I had seen her.

"Jensen, do you see her?" Connor asked, frightened.

"No!"

I saw my mom and dad jump off their boards into the water to look for her. I did the same and began looking. My vision was blurred, and my eyes burned from the saltwater. When I saw her, she looked like an angel. Her hair was wavy all over underneath the water. I swam toward her. When I took her hand, I saw something that looked like black smoke attached to her leg.

"We've lost Jensen now," Maya said. "Nathaniel, over here!"

"Connor, swim to shore now," Nathaniel said firmly.

"But, Nathaniel, I can help."

"Not today, son. Now go swim to shore as fast as you can. Find help!" Nathaniel said, swimming over to Maya.

"Where did Jensen go under?" Nathaniel urgently asked.

"He was right here, but I don't see him now."

"Nathaniel, you don't think."

"Never mind that. We have to find them. The balance of everything lies with those two," Nathaniel said, diving into the water.

I started having trouble holding my breath. I could feel the water begin entering my lungs. Feeling them build up with pressure, I began to become weak. I was losing consciousness. Still holding on to Octavia's hand tight, I began to panic. I tried to swim up to the surface, but the black smoke would not let her free. I flicked my wrist, and the Nevillin appeared. I hit the black smoke. It sounded as if it let out a faint scream. When it disappeared, I began swimming toward the surface as fast as I could, holding on to Octavia.

"Nathaniel, over there!" Maya shouted as she and Nathaniel swam toward us.

"Dad, she's not breathing." I panicked as I put my hand on her chest.

"We need to get her to shore. Give her to me, Jensen."

When Nathaniel took her, he went underneath the water. With her cradled in both arms, I saw him take off like a rocket underneath the water, leaving his surfboard behind. Suddenly, something grabbed my leg and pulled me under. It was the black smoke again. I flicked my wrist, and the Nevillin appeared. I swung it at the black smoke. This time, it blocked my katana with what appeared to be a spear. Throwing a jab at me, it stabbed me in the shoulder. Letting out a faint cry, I lunged back at it with the Nevillin, striking it, then it disappeared. Trying to swim to the surface, another one grabbed my leg and pulled me under. I again became weak. Pulling me deeper, I saw my mom reaching down for me. With her katana in hand, she hit the black smoke, and it disappeared. As we swam to the surface, I could see the sun piercing through the water. Breaking through the surface of the water, I took a deep breath of air. Mom and I began swimming as fast as we could toward the shore. As we got closer, I could see Connor sitting on the beach next to Octavia while my dad and a lifeguard were administering CPR. Running out of the ocean, I fell to my knees next to my dad. Taking Octavia's hand, I began to weep. I felt like a child again as tears filled my eyes. My mom came from behind me and draped herself over me, holding me tight.

"Please, God, don't take her," I begged out loud, sobbing.

"Sir, I'm sorry, there's nothing more we can do," the lifeguard said to Nathaniel softly, taking a towel and placing it over her face.

"No, no, no, no!" I began to whimper and sob.

"Jensen, she's gone," Maya said, holding me tight.

"Oh my God, this isn't happening. Take me. Please take me!" I begged, looking to the sky.

"Take you. Please take, you say?" a raspy voice whispered.

"Who said that?" I asked softly, closing my eyes.

"I go by many names. You may call me Rayzeal. I am known as the crossroads Jinn. The one and only of my kind," the raspy voice whispered. "What deal are you prepared to make to bring your loved one back?"

"Anything."

"Anything, you say? What about your body, your life?"

"You bring her back. It's yours."

"Awake, Octavia, someone else has taken your place," the raspy voice whispered.

Just then, Octavia sat up, spitting up water and coughing.

"Jensen, what did you do?" Maya asked, super worried.

"I had to."

"Jensen, do you have your crucifix?"

"Yes," I said as I reached to feel it under my wetsuit.

"Jensen, stay close to Octavia and Connor. The two of you, hold her and keep her warm."

"Sir, an ambulance is on the way," the lifeguard said.

"Nathaniel, we have a problem. Jensen made a deal with a Jinn," Maya said, worried.

"We have other problems. They are no longer just looking for Jensen," Nathaniel said as he looked at Octavia and Connor.

I watched as my parents walked over to the shoreline on the beach. They looked out over the ocean with concern and whispered to each other.

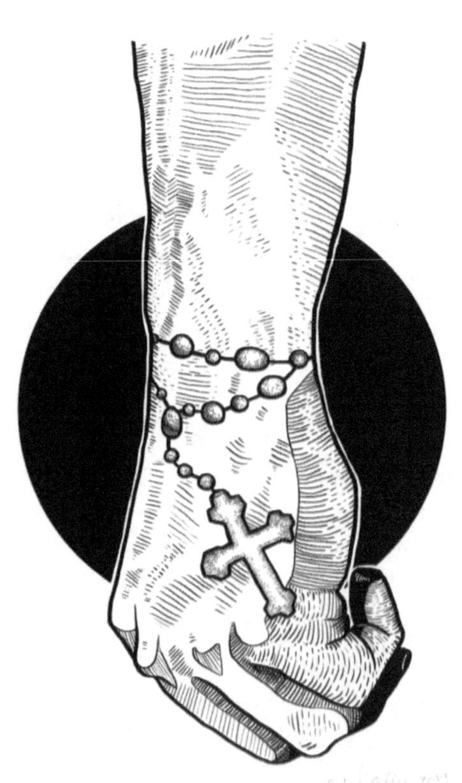

Jensen's Fate

Jensen

It's been three years to the day since we were attacked in the ocean by the Jinn. Rayzeal, the Jinn I made the deal with to save Octavia, I often thought "did he forget about me?" I sealed my fate that day, and I knew it was only a matter of time before he would come to collect. Nathaniel took the cross he gave me when I was just a boy and had it crafted into three separate crosses. Giving one to each—Octavia, Connor, and I. I turned mine into a bracelet, using beads from an old rosary that had been given to me by Alyssa Kryst. What I didn't expect was it to adhere itself to me. The day I put it around my left hand, it turned into a tattoo and was now permanent; I remember how bad it hurt and how sore it was for days.

When I started my senior year back at Dana Hills High School. I had become quarterback after the previous starting quarterback graduated. I had been a wide receiver in my first three previous years at school. I had put on a significant amount of muscle mass over the summer by hitting the gym hard. My girlfriend, Octavia Kryst, was envied by all the girls at school, and every boy wanted to be me. Our grades were all flawless; and Octavia, Connor, and I were all geared to becoming valedictorians.

But as fate would have it, after about four months into school, Rayzeal began creeping into my life. He'd make me feel lost and empty at times. My temper was like a roller coaster, and at the slightest insult or trite remark, I could fly into a violent temper. I knew this wasn't me but Rayzeal coming out. His raspy voice would echo in my head. My mind became plagued by him as he began invading it. I would get what I thought were premonitions at times and become paranoid about my family's whereabouts and safety. When I saw him for the first time in a nightmare, he appeared as black smoke. His eyes were empty and pierced themselves into my mind. In my nightmares he would often, kill those I loved with a bloodied meat cleaver the size of a man's torso or a spear covered in fresh blood and flesh would be hanging from it. He would hang them from crosses and as they'd cry out in pain he'd torture them further by whipping them with a barbed wire whip. He began whispering things to me about what he'd like to do to Octavia. I became so paranoid that I lost sleep and found comfort in the darkness and found myself staring off into it. Sometimes I'd fall asleep in class, and it would only be for a moment. But to me, that moment would feel like hours.

"Mr. Kane, Mr. Kane, Jensen Kane!" the history teacher said, slamming a book on my desk, waking me up.

"Holy shit!" I said, startled, rubbing my eyes.

"Don't fall asleep in my class."

"Well, maybe I wouldn't if your class wasn't so boring."

"What did you just say?"

"Ooooh, look at that, saved by the bell," I said as the bell rang and I walked out of class.

"Hey, babe," Octavia said, waiting outside my class. "Gee, you look really tired. Are you okay?"

"Hey, you two," Connor said, walking up to Octavia and I in the hallway. "Should we bounce off campus today for lunch?"

"Anything sounds better than hanging around here," Octavia replied.

"Jensen, let's take your truck," Connor said.

Jumping in the truck, we drove off campus to Z Pizza, that was located at Ocean Ranch Plaza, where many other students from school enjoyed hanging out in between class periods and on the weekends. I had a job working as an assistant manager at a movie theater.

"Yo, Octavia. What's up?" a boy from our school said whom I knew to be on the surf team with Octavia.

"Hey, Julian," Octavia replied as Julian hugged her after we jumped out of the truck.

"Jensen, what's up?" Julian asked. "I heard you're starting quarterback this year. Maybe our school will actually have a chance now of winning. The last quarterback sucked with all the interceptions he threw last year. You should have joined the surf team with Octavia and I. She tells me you're better than most of the students on the team."

"Well there's still time. I may join you," I said looking around.

"Bring it, man. It would be nice getting better competition out there," Julian said playfully nudging Octavia.

"What about me, Julian?" Connor said. "I'm not enough competition for you?"

"Connor, you'll always be my boy, but most of the girls are better than you," Julian said, laughing before hugging Connor. "Nah, I'm just joking, bro."

"Well, I'll talk to you guys later. Have a good one," Julian said as he hugged Octavia and walked back over to his friends.

"Damn, Julian, she's hot. That must be awesome to hug her on the beach at surfing practice. Her perfect body and those perfect tits of hers smashing up against you," a friend of Julian's said as he walked over to them.

"Don't talk about her like that, Juan. That's her boyfriend right there," Julian replied. "Show some respect."

"You tapping that shit, dog?" Juan asked like a pervert loud enough for us to hear. "Yeah! You tapping that, right?"

"Motherfucker," I said grinding my teeth, turning around to walk over to them.

"Jensen," Octavia softly said, putting her hand on my chest and shaking her head. "He's not worth it."

"Who is that with Julian?" I asked Connor.

"Ah, that idiot. His name is Juan Martinez. He's a known gang member of the San Juan Disciples. Apparently, he was expelled last year for bringing a weapon to school."

While we were eating and hanging out outside Z Pizza, I kept seeing this Juan character looking at the three of us. When we were done eating and began walking out to my truck, Juan and a couple of his friends approached us.

"What's up, dog?" he said as I opened the door to my truck, saying nothing. "What, you too good to say anything, bitch?"

"Yeah, but I'm not too good to put your face into the pavement," I said as he kicked the door of my truck shut. "You really want to do this? I'll clean this parking lot with your dead fuckin' body," I said, getting in his face.

"Is that a fact?" He asked trying to intimidate me.

"It's a promise."

"All right, enough!" Octavia shouted, getting in between us.

"Who the fuck are you, bitch?" Juan sneered.

"Such big words for such a tough guy," Octavia said.

"Bitch, you know who you're fuckin with?" Juan shouted as he and his posse became angered further.

"A boy with extremely high testosterone." Octavia shrugged. "If you don't mind, we're leaving now."

"On the contrary we do mind," Juan said getting in Octavia's face.

"Juan! What's your problem, man," Julian said running up.

"Jensen," Octavia said steering me away from Juan as I continued to stare he and his weak little posse down. "Jensen!" she shouted getting my attention on her.

"He's not worth it, baby. Walk away," she smiled as we all jumped in my truck and returned to school.

"Jensen, what's wrong?" Connor asked as we pulled up to the school and I rubbed my head.

"I'm fine. I just wanna go home."

"What's the matter?" Octavia asked.

"I just don't feel like going to class."

"All right, just take care of yourself and don't do anything stupid," Octavia said, concerned. "I'll come by and check on you after school."

"All right."

"Look at me," Octavia said, grabbing my face and looking into my eyes. "Don't do anything stupid," she said sternly. "I know you better then you know yourself and you've got that look in your eye."

"I won't," I said continuing to rub my head. "I promise."

"Okay."

When I walked in the front door of my house, there was a breeze that came at me. It was sturdy and echoed through the house. Calling out to see if anyone was home, I got no answer. Finally, I heard a voice. It was soft but raspy. It was Rayzeal. His voice was deeper and raspier than normal as if he were close. Walking into the bathroom I splashed water on my face and looked in the mirror.

"I've waited a long time, Jensen Kane," an image of myself in a mirror said in Rayzeal's raspy voice. "We had a deal, boy. It's time to pay up," Rayzeal said. "You remember our deal, don't you?"

"I do, Rayzeal, and I'll honor it. But I'll be damned if I'm going to make it easy for you to take me," I said, arguing. "Who are you, Rayzeal?"

"Soon you and I will be the same, Jensen Kane. You'll be me. I'll be you. Soon we'll know more about each other than we ever cared to know. I tell you, though, the one thing I'm really looking forward to about being you is screwing that hottie of yours," Rayzeal said, laughing. "Tell me, Jensen, is she still ripe, or have you already broken her in?"

"If you . . ."

"If I what? You may live among the humans, but you will never be one no matter how hard you try. You can't escape who you really are. That's why I'm here. To make sense of it for you. We will bring them death. And soon I'll wreak havoc upon all those you love. I know you care for her, boy, and she will be the one hurt most, I promise. How do you think she will feel when she finds out that you made a deal?" Rayzeal laughed. "And then there's Nathaniel, who I know all too well. Soon he will feel the same pain as you, and all this will be gone. Soon they will all feel our wrath, right, Jensen? Or should I call you Spraygin?"

"Enough, Rayzeal!" I flicked my wrist and shouted, looking into the bathroom mirror.

"Are you challenging me, boy?" my reflection said. "To kill me is to kill yourself."

"Then so be it."

"Let me teach you a lesson, boy," Rayzeal said, walking out of the mirror in physical form.

Without hesitation, I quickly flicked my wrist, and when the Nevillin appeared, I attacked. Coming at him with everything I had, he caught me off guard and punched me in the chest. Falling to my knees, he lunged at me with a spear. When I blocked it with the Nevillin, I quickly came up and punched him in the face. As I stood up, he looked at me, laughed, and disappeared before the doorbell rang. Standing up I brushed myself off and went to answer the door.

"Hey, babe," Octavia said as I opened the door and she walked in. "How are you feeling?"

"Octavia, I have to tell you something," I said, taking her hand in mine. "The day we were attacked in the ocean . . ." I said and hesitated.

"What, babe? What is it?"

"You died," I blurted out.

"I died," Octavia repeated. "That doesn't make sense."

"It does. I made a deal with a Jinn to reverse your fate."

"You took onto yourself my fate?"

"What are you guys discussing?" Nathaniel asked, walking in through the garage.

"Dad, I need to talk to you."

"I know of the deal you made, Jensen," Nathaniel said. "The only reason this Jinn has not been able to take you yet is because you are stronger than him. The Jinn needs you to fear him if he is to possess you. What is the name of the Jinn that haunts you?"

"Rayzeal."

"That sounds familiar."

"It said it knows you."

"It would say anything at this point. It's becoming desperate."

"But why now?"

"I'm not sure, but you're not alone in this. We'll find out together," he said looking at Octavia and I.

The Possession

Nathaniel

As the days passed, Maya and I watched as Jensen fell into a bitter depression. His moods became stranger than normal. His school began calling us with concern about his behavior and sending concerning letters about his attendance and absolute disregard for policy and authority. I turned to the Elder Grimoire for answers on how to deal with the Jinn who called himself Rayzeal. The name sounded awfully familiar, but I couldn't put my finger on it. Maya looked as if she knew something but wasn't saying. I began reading an entry in the Elder Grimoire about a young girl whom Everin counseled in the abyss. It read as if the Elder Grimoire had recorded the conversation word for word.

> "My name is Guya. My dreams and thoughts were plagued by a nightmarish creature named Azrael who referred to himself as a crossroads Jinn. Just talking about him again brings back only the worst of memories. He would taunt me to do evil things. The more I resisted, the more I fell into his evil grasp. It wasn't till he taunted me to murder my parents that I made

a different evil decision. I took my own life in fear that he would kill them and use my hands as the instruments. I remember when my parents found me in their bathtub; they were so disappointed and upset. I looked down on them from the bright light that held my soul up; I saw how I broke their hearts. I saw my limp, lifeless body being held by my father. I was finally rid of Azrael but at the cost of my life. It was then I saw Everin. She smiled at me and told me, 'God forgives you, Guya. Bring your sins to me and forgive yourself.'"

"Guya, I have had many sessions speaking with you. Though you may be rid of Azrael, if I were to grant you reincarnation and a crossroads Jinn were to return, how would you approach him this time around?"

"I would confront him."

"You would confront him?"

"Yes, I would wait till he would haunt me in a nightmare, and there I would confront him and show him no fear."

"Guya, you fought with him already once over your soul, and you said the more you fought him, the more powerful he became over you," Everin said.

"Yes but while I was fighting him I always showed fear and in doing so I fueled the fire for him to become powerful over me. I took the easy way out. Fear was what he craved, and that's what he needed to take me, my fear. Showing me awful things was how he got me to fear him. My parents dead by my own hands," Guya explained. "This is my life. They're my dreams, my nightmares. I would tell him that he is not welcome in them and that he won't find anyone here that fears him."

"How do you know this would work?"

"I don't, but I can imagine that since this is my life and my body, I would have more power than him."

"Jensen needs to confront him," I said to myself aloud holding the Elder Grimoire.

"Nathaniel, who are you talking to?" Maya asked, walking into the study.

"I was just talking out loud."

"Did you find anything?"

"Jensen needs to confront Rayzeal. It's fear Rayzeal craves. It's fear that makes him strong," I said to Maya. "Where is Jensen, now?"

"He should be at school, Nathaniel."

"His truck is here," I said, looking out the window.

"So what are we talking about?" Jensen said in a raspy voice, holding the Nevillin and walking into the study. "Ah, reverting to the book of lies, are we?"

"Rayzeal. Or should I call you Azrael?"

"So you've heard of me?" Azrael smiled and asked.

"I have, Azrael," I said never taking my eye off him. "Everin recorded it all right here in the book you refer to as, the book of lies."

"Of course she did."

"So you know what I'll do if you try to take him from me."

"You Jinn are all the same," Maya said as I flicked my wrist.

"You will fail. Just like Everin failed to save Guya."

"That's not true. Everin did save Guya," I said confused.

"Is that what your precious Grimoire says?" Azrael said and smiled sinisterly. "Reincarnation. It's a bitch, isn't it? Granted to those the Elders found worthy to go back and make all new mistakes and fuck it up again."

"Quiet, Jinn!" I shouted.

"Godric is gone, and soon his precious grandson will be too," Azrael said, smirking. "Tell me, Nathaniel, will you run like a coward the way Godric did?"

"Zeyreal?" I said confused, *thinking this couldn't of been the same Jinn I have dealt with on many different occasions. Or could it?*

"Zeyreal, Rayzeal, Azrael I have so many names. You may call me by whatever name you prefer."

"Jensen, believe in God. Pray to him. He will bring you strength. Show Azrael no fear!" Nathaniel shouted.

"He's not here anymore! You're talking to a ghost," Azrael mocked.

"Soon Jensen will join Guya."

"You can't win, Azrael. Jensen is stronger than you," Maya said as Azrael swung the Nevillin and Maya blocked it. "And you know it."

"We'll see," Azrael said as he ran out the front door.

"Should we go after him?" Maya said, concerned.

"No, there's nothing we can do. We have to believe Jensen heard us. He's the only one now that can stop this." I sighed. "We must have faith in Jensen."

"Faith? Prayers to God? God can no longer hear us, Nathaniel. It's time to give it up. They're dead! They're all dead! You keep clinging to this hope that he might still be alive. None of them are coming back. Why can't you just accept it as I have? Any faith we have now is hollow," Maya said, upset as I turned away to walk out the door and stopped.

"He's still alive, Maya," I said.

"Who, Nathaniel? God, Godric, whatever you want to call him," Maya said, shrugging her shoulders. "How do you know?"

"I have faith, Maya. It's all I need. Every time I look at Jensen, I see . . . him. I see Everin. I see their spirit flowing through that boy," I said, taking a deep breath. "I'll never give up my faith. It's a part of me, and it always will be," I said before walking out of the room.

Jensen

Suddenly, I heard the bell ring. Picking up my head from the desk, I looked around and saw that I was in my music class.

"Nice of you to join us again, Mr. Kane," Mr. Shepherd said as everyone but Octavia began walking out of class.

"How did I get here?" I responded, surprised to be in class.

"Well, you came in late and then fell asleep," Mr. Shepherd said with a disappointed look on his face."

"I'm sorry," I said, taking a deep breath and standing up.

"Jensen, I'm really concerned. Your grade has dropped in my class significantly. You're one of my brightest students, and you have such a gift."

"I'm sorry, Mr. Shepherd. I just haven't been myself lately."

"I would say so. Whatever's going on in your life, you need to get it straightened out, son."

"I will, Mr. Shepherd, and again, I'm sorry," I said, walking out of class with Octavia.

When I opened the classroom door, I hit Cesar Martinez in the face. Cesar was a known gang affiliate of the San Juan Capistrano Disciples and was not someone to be trifled with.

"What the fuck, ese?" one of Cesar's friends shouted.

"Sorry, are you okay?" I asked.

"That's all you can say?" the friend replied still angry.

"It was just an accident," Octavia said frustrated.

"One word from me, and I could have you killed."

"I doubt that," I said rolling my eye's mocking them.

"Are you trying to insult us?" Cesar asked, getting up off the floor and into my face.

"He asked if you're okay and you deem that offensive." Octavia said shaking her head. "My God, you disciples are ignorant."

"Jensen, Octavia," Connor said, walking up to me, grabbing our arms. "Let's go, guys."

"You've got all your little bitches stepping in for you don't you Mr. Quarterback?" Cesar said.

"Who you calling a bitch, motherfucker?" Connor said, turning around, shoving Cesar.

"No, Connor!" Octavia said, pulling Connor away as Cesar shoved him back, causing Octavia to fall and he and his friends busted up laughing.

"Motherfucker!" I shouted in a raspy voice, slugging Cesar.

"Damn, Jensen! You just love hitting these disciple bitches, don't you?" Connor said, laughing, while Cesar held his nose with blood coming out from in between his fingers. "You know you've managed to hit two disciples within forty-eight hours and break both their noses."

"Yeah, not to mention their brothers," Octavia added.

"Well, now they're twins," I said, looking down at him. "How about you guys? You want some too?"

"You boys stop that now!" a teacher shouted, walking up to us.

"We'll finish this later, puto!" a disciple with Cesar shouted.

"Walk away, Cesar. Go to the nurse's office. Now!" the teacher said, angry. "How come whenever there's a problem I find you three at the end of it?"

"Well, mam, Jensen here . . . ahh, he just attracts violence," Connor said, mocking the teacher.

"Funny man, ah, Mr. Kryst?"

"What can I say, it comes naturally, mam," Connor said, smiling.

"Well, Mr. Kryst, I'm sure you can naturally find your way to the principal's office."

"Naturally," Connor said with a big grin, grabbing Octavia and I by the arms. "But I must decline. I'll be going with my friends now."

"Connor Kryst, you will be getting a call at home," the teacher said firmly.

"Good luck with that," Connor said as we all walked out of school. "So, Jensen, how'd you get into it with that idiot?" Connor asked, smirking.

"I opened a door, and it hit him."

"That's great," Connor said and laughed. "Did you hear about how these disciples are initiating people into their gang?"

"No," I said, annoyed.

"They're beginning to make the news. Two of their recruits jumped a pregnant woman last week at a gas station. They took turns stabbing her in the stomach before running off with her purse."

"My God, that's awful," Octavia said shocked.

"I know, tell me about it."

"Hey, guys, I'll get back at you later."

"Jensen, where are you going?" Connor asked, worried.

"Jensen!" Octavia concerned

"Leave me alone, Octavia," I said in a raspy voice before turning my head to crack my neck.

"Jensen. What's up with you, man?" Connor asked as I walked away. "What's his problem?" Connor asked looking at Octavia.

"I don't know," Octavia said. "I have to get to my next class."

"Did his voice just change? He must be getting sick. That raspy voice of his just came out of nowhere," Connor said talking to himself. "Maybe it's puberty?" Connor said thinking. "That would explain the mood swings," Connor said smiling and walking to class.

The rest of the day was a blur. I felt sick to my stomach and drowsy. When the end of school came, I took off in my truck and ignored every attempt Octavia and Connor made to try to talk to me throughout the day. Driving away, I looked at them in my rearview mirror. Suddenly, I saw a group of about seven disciples run into the parking lot at them. I saw Connor get blindsided and hit directly in the side of the face. Octavia dropped her bag and began fighting. Flipping my truck around, I sped back into the parking lot of the school. Smashing up against a parked Honda Civic, I threw the truck in park. I jumped out and grabbed two of the seven disciples who were stacking up on Connor. Throwing one of them up against a parked car, I turned the other around and saw it was Juan Martinez, Cesar's older brother. Feeling anger flow through my veins, I began punching him in the face over and over till his body became limp. Dropping him to the ground, I engaged the one I had thrown up against the parked car. Holding him by his hair, I began pummeling his face. Not before long, I was being pulled off him by Connor and Octavia. Looking around, I saw the disciples who had not run off standing around Juan. His face was bloodied, battered, and swollen. He looked like he had gotten hit by a freight train.

"He's dead," one of his fellow disciples said, alarmed and shocked.

"Jensen, look at me," Octavia said, grabbing my face to look at her. "It was self-defense. They attacked us. You didn't do anything wrong."

My hands began to shake. "It's not the same feeling as killing Jinn," I said as my hands continued to shake. "He's dead. I killed him. I have to go," I said in a raspy voice.

"Where, Jensen? Where're you gonna go?" Octavia said, firmly shaking her head.

"What's up with your voice?" Connor asked.

"Forget his voice, Connor!" Octavia said. "Jensen, leaving isn't the answer. It was self-defense. We were jumped."

"I have go."

"Jensen, don't do this!" Octavia demanded.

"I'm not safe for anyone. Danger is all around me, all the time. It haunts me like a plague. This would've never happened had I not gotten into it with him."

"Stay away from me, Octavia."

"Jensen, I don't understand," Octavia said as I turned to walk away.

"You don't need to," I said, continuing to walk away. "This is my problem. I'll deal with it."

"You can't leave like this, Jensen," Connor said, stepping in front of me.

"Get the fuck out of my way," I said, mad.

"Or else what, Jensen? You gonna hit me too?"

"I told you to move," I said, grabbing Connor by the shirt and throwing him to the ground.

Jumping in my truck, I drove home. Bursting through the door of my house, I ran upstairs to my room. Dumping everything out from my backpack, I began packing it with clothes. I couldn't believe I killed him. Worst of all, I was unsure of how I felt about it, and that scared me.

"You know you enjoyed killing him, Jensen. Stop lying to yourself," Azrael said in a raspy voice.

"Leave me the fuck alone, Azrael."

"You remember this morning, don't you?"

"I remember everything."

"When are you going to come to terms with what you really are?"

"And what's that?"

"A killer!"

"No."

"No. Then what do you call what you just did, pummeling that poor boy's face in?"

"That was you, Azrael, not me."

"You don't truly believe that," Azrael said, laughing. "It's your basic killer instinct, boy, and if it were me that had done that, I would have ripped off their limbs. You lost control, seeing them attack your loved ones. Better yet, let me show you what I would've done."

I felt cold, and my vision became gray and blurred. I could see my hands and feet, but I had no control over myself. Looking down at the Sigil on my bicep, I watched as it began to glow bright red. This was when I knew the possession had come full circle and I was no longer in control.

"Jensen, are you home?" Maya said, walking in the front door downstairs.

"You hear that, boy?" Azrael said, excited and raspy. "Time to kill this bitch once and for all."

"Don't do this, Azrael. I'll do whatever you want me to."

"Oh, Jensen, it's too late for that. Let's show Mommy her little monster. Now, shoosh, I have killing to do."

Azrael flicked his wrist. When the Nevillin appeared, he crept out from Jensen's room and looked over the balcony. With a running start, he sprang off the balcony and came down at Maya, swinging the Nevillin. Maya, knowing something was wrong, flicked her wrist. When her katana appeared, she blocked the Nevillin.

"Azrael," Maya said, angered.

"I'm sorry, Mommy, but you must die now," Azrael said, grinning.

"What have you done with my son?" Maya said, keeping her guard up.

"Your son? Last time I checked, you aren't even the real mother. What's it like knowing that? Playing mommy is all you'll ever know. I hope you enjoyed it while it lasted because that's over now, but nothing to worry about, I'll take very good care of him. He has joined Guya now."

"Jensen, listen to me. You have to fight him and show him no fear. Have faith. You're stronger than him, and he knows it."

"Shut your mouth, bitch!" Azrael shouted, taking a swing at Maya.

"Jensen fight him. The only reason he's able to wield the Nevillin is because you allow him to. The Nevillin is the source of your power. Take it!" Azrael came at Maya, swinging the Nevillin relentlessly till it suddenly disappeared.

"He's mine!" Azrael shouted before turning and jumping out a nearby window.

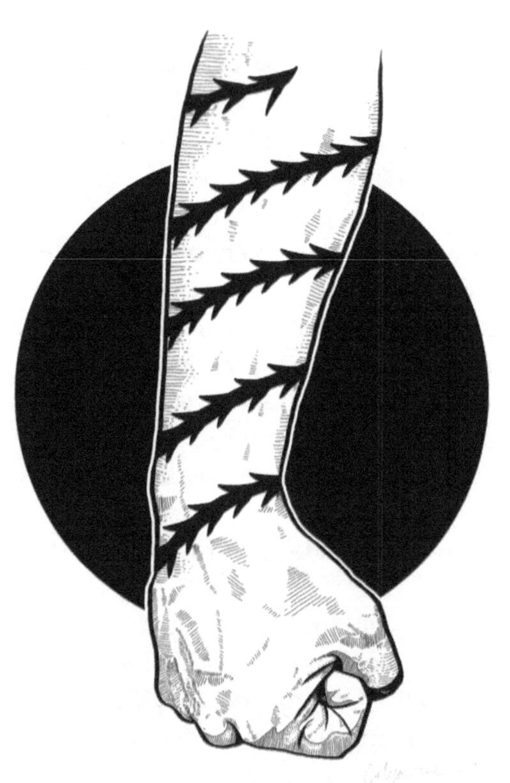

Finding Enreal

Jensen

It was cold, windy, and raining. Everything was blurred and gray. I couldn't see myself anymore as I looked down. It was as if I didn't exist anymore. I closed my jacket and zipped it up, thinking, *How did I get here? What is this place? How could I've become so lost that Azrael would be able to take my life and make it his own?* In a lot of ways I felt sorry for him, but why? Why feel sorry for a Jinn? Feeling sorry for him opened me up to his attack which made me his victim and opened me up to his possession.

As I walked, my feet felt heavy and tired. I could hear my mom's voice echoing in the darkness, telling me to fight, but why could I still hear her? Was her voice in my head? Is this something I wanted to hear, or was this truly her on the other side, fighting Azrael? Every step I took, I would call out to Azrael, hoping he would answer, but he never did. As I rubbed my eyes, the blurriness began to fade. This place that was once gray now became color. The rain continued to pour, and the wind continued to howl. This place looked like home, but it was dark, torn and battered. The wind and rain were unnatural, and I could sense something elusive, something supernatural all around me. The evil in this place was very strong.

"Beware the weeping widow," a soft voice over the wind warned.

"Are you okay?" I asked a girl who I saw sitting on the ground, nude and crying, my voice still raspy, like Azrael's.

"We're waiting for him." an evil voice said.

"Who's him?" I replied.

"The one."

"The one?" I repeated, confused.

"The one we've been waiting for. The tortured soul, Spraygin," the evil voice said as if it were coming from the nude girl.

"I'm Spraygin."

"I've been waiting a long time for you. To understand Azrael is to understand oneself," the evil voice continued saying. "Azrael is Spraygin. Spraygin is Azrael. You are he. He is you. Azrael, Jensen, Spraygin, you."

"What are you?" I asked, looking at the nude girl.

"This place is you. So you tell me. What am I?" the girl said, turning around, looking at me with empty, lifeless eyes.

"Mom," I said and fell to my knees next to her.

"There is no mom here. Look at your greatest fear. Fear is here. Fear in doubt of yourself," she said as she took my hands.

"Mom, listen to me. Your name is Maya. You're the highest of all angels. You're an elder. Don't you remember? Remember Nathaniel?" I asked as she began to weep.

"Nathaniel," she said confused in thought.

"Yeah, Mom, Nathaniel." I said sympathetic.

"I'm here because of him. His lies were too much."

"What?" I said as she placed my hands them on her face with my thumbs resting where her eyes once were.

I saw dark things coming in flashes. I saw myself on top of a world covered in blood, and I was responsible for all of its destruction. I saw Jinn rallied behind me and the world in fear and chaos. Connor was shackled in chains with hooks pierced through the skin of his back, suspended. My parents lay dead in front of me. I had slit their throats with a katana unfamiliar to me. I had given Octavia to Jinn warriors to be raped and tortured. All this was done by my hand.

"No!" I shouted, pulling my hands away from Maya. "This won't happen!"

"How sure are you? Spraygin, Jensen, Azrael. Destruction, chaos, death."

Suddenly I heard the true voice of my mother shouting "the Nevillin is the source of your power, take it!"

"This is my life, my world. I'll forge whatever future I wish," I said as I flicked my wrist and the Nevillin appeared.

"No!" the entity impersonating Maya screamed before vanishing.

Continuing on I began seeing broken-down cars and buildings in flames with falling debris as the wind and the rain faded away. I saw what looked like Jinn trying to catch something. When I ran over to where I had seen them, I saw in a ritualistic manner an owl being held down to a stone with a flat surface while its wings were spread apart with barbed wire. As soon as I saw a Jinn pull out a hatchet I knew then they were going to cut the wings off of this beautiful creature. Running at them with the Nevillin, I swung at them, and like cowards they vanished.

When I looked down, there on the ground was this owl. It was a light tan with brown and light blue feathers throughout its coat.

"Let me help you," I said to the owl, unwinding the barbed wire that was wrapped around its wings.

"Thank you, Jensen," the owl said as I jumped up, surprised.

"How are you able to do that?" I asked, shocked that it could speak.

"Do what?" the owl asked.

"Talk."

"You understand me through your ability to use telepathy."

"Telepathy?"

"It's an ability that only the Goodwater family possesses."

"How did you come to be in this place?" I asked.

"That's a long story."

"What is this place?"

"Purgatory."

"Purgatory. You mean we're stuck between life and death?"

"Unfortunately."

"How do I know I can trust you?" I said looking around. "Look at this place. It's filled with nothing but evil. How do I know this isn't a trick?"

"I will forever serve the family of the Kane's and Goodwater's this is the oath I made and I am forever bound to you and Enreal."

"Enreal!" I said shocked. "She's here?"

"She's been here stuck and waiting for you to. I will take you to her."

"How'd the two of you become stuck here?" I asked as we began walking.

Lost her way a bit, but you can both help one another escape this horrible place."

"Enreal's sigil is branded on the blade of my katana."

"So you know how important it is that she survives this place?"

I do.

"Where can I find her?"

"Follow me."

"How is it that you two became separated here?

"That's a long story."

"What's your name?" I asked curious but polite.

"Tigist."

"I remember reading about you in the Elder Grimoire. You and Jesus were close."

"He and I were inseparable. Much like Enreal and I. Our lives are tied to one another," Tigist looked deep in thought. "What happens to her happens to me."

Walking over to the broken-down truck. I didn't know what to expect. I saw a young girl sitting on a log in front of a small fire.

"Enreal?" Tigist said softly.

"Tigist"

"It's me."

"Who's that with you?" Enreal asked, looking over her shoulder at me.

"He's a friend"

"I brought him to you so you can once again remember who you are and what you stand for. Regain your honor. We're not dying in this place."

"Tigist, we don't even know what this place is."

"It's purgatory, and Dad is at your bedside right now. But if we don't do something soon, we'll be lost here forever."

"What if your new friend here is one of those things?"

"What things?" I asked.

"See those things at the top of that building circling around it? Those are reapers, shape-shifting creatures. They can mimic those you love to anything you may loathe. They are vile creatures very similar to Jinn more difficult to kill."

"Is that the elder grimoire?" I asked, seeing it sitting on the log alongside her.

Quickly standing up, Enreal grabbed a thick dried out tree branch and she swung it at me. Dodging it, I flicked my wrist. When the Nevillin appeared, I began fighting her. Her form in swordsmanship was identical to my own. It was as if she and I were connected. When I broke the branch down to nothing, she flicked her wrists, and two guns appeared. Dodging the shots, it was as if she knew all my moves before I did and her form when wielding these guns was like art in motion, it was beautiful. After many attempts, one of the bullets hit my leg.

"That's enough!" Tigist shouted, flying in between us as I fell to the ground holding my leg in pain.

"Touchy about this one, hmm?" Enreal said as she knelt down, putting her hand over the bullet wound on my leg. Watching it heal instantly, I knew this was no ordinary girl.

"You have no idea how important he is, young lady. From now on, you will do what I say. Understand?" Tigist said to Enreal firmly. "Do you understand me?"

"Where did you learn to fight like that?" I asked.

"My father taught me."

"Did he also teach you how to fight with guns?"

"It's called gun kata."

"Yes!" Enreal shouted getting angry.

"Now, hand him the grimoire," Tigist said.

"Here," she said as she grabbed it and threw it at my feet.

Suddenly, a heavy cloud cover came over us, accompanied by a strong gust of wind. The grimoire flipped open to a page, and there before my eyes, I saw Enreal in sadness as I saw visions of her past and how she came to be in this place. Tears were pouring down her face while she was writing in the elder grimoire and her tears began to soak into the pages and the story was told.

My name is Enreal. If you're reading this, it means that I'm dead and no longer a burden to this world. To better understand how I came to the decision of taking my own life, I would need to tell you about how I came to be in the dark place I am. I thought it would only be fitting to write this short chapter of my life in the Elder Grimoire as it's the book that chronicles my family's origin.

I was born in Dana Point, California. I don't remember much of those early years, but I do remember often gazing at the clouds and wondering if Godric was still up there. Before I was born my mother had a successful career in the music industry and became quite an icon. She was revered by many for being an extreme philanthropist. It wasn't till I was born that she fell into a coma only to never wake up. When I was thirteen I found myself attracted to a girl named Ruth. I remember questioning my thoughts but the way the sun touched her hair, I had never seen someone so beautiful. I thought we would love each other forever. I remember our teacher telling us it was just an adolescent phase that we would outgrow. Ruth did; I didn't.

When I met Valerie it was as if time stopped and everything stood still. It was in my high school music class. I was aspiring to become as great as a singer as my mother. Valerie played the cello. I could listen to her play for hours I could hear every note. The first time we kissed, I knew I never wanted to kiss anyone but her again. She became my everything. That was also when I came out to my father. He was accepting of my choices and supported my actions. Valerie's parents repudiated her and made her feel ashamed. Much like Valerie's parents, there were people out there who hated us.

I had always known what I wanted to do with my life. I reformed my parents legendary symphonic metal band, Embrace the Fate with myself taking over lead vocals. It was a beautiful time in my life where everything was falling into place and I was so happy I had someone to share my life with, Valerie. Our love story was imbedded in the house we bought together that over looked my beautiful ocean. We would surf every day and work in our atrium where we grew Jasmine in Gardenia flowers and our place always smelled beautiful..

But as fate would have it, all I was left with were blissful memories of a life that was taken from me. In an instant, my life changed forever, and she was gone, taken from me. I never cried so hard in my life. After this, our once beautiful home became as I did—dead inside, broken, and empty. I isolated myself from everyone and everything and apologized for nothing.

It seems strange that my life should end this way. But for all the years I had with Valerie, all I knew was love and happiness.

I shall die here now, alone, broken, and empty. Never fearing, never forgiving, and never forgetting. Everything I once was is gone now in the blink of an eye. Everything I believed in perished. I'm broken and lost without you Valerie. The last thing my soul will ever feel again are the knives of Trivium. I leave this world of my own free will with no apologies.

"Valerie went to the grocery store. I remember a few minutes after she left, getting a bad feeling that something was wrong. Leaving about three minutes behind her, I got to the store, but I was too late. I walked in, and everyone in the store was being butchered like cattle by Jinn, and there standing over Valerie was a female Jinn dressed in all black with a katana pierced through her chest. I flicked my wrist, my katana appeared, and I began slaying all the Jinn in my path till I reached the female Jinn. Dodging and blocking everything I threw at her, she suddenly vanished in a black smoke, along with her minions. I fell to my knees next to Valerie, picking her up gently I placed her head on my thighs I could see that she was having trouble breathing. The severity of her wound was beyond repair. I had her blood all over me. She was coughing up and drowning in it when I tried healing her. It must have been too late, and she was too far gone. I could do nothing but hold her and tell her I loved her," Enreal said as her eyes filled with tears.

"She kept gasping for air and telling me she couldn't breathe. I couldn't do anything. I wasn't able to save her. I blamed myself for the danger I put her in. She's dead because of me. All I wanted was to join her in death. I slit my wrists on my katana," Enreal said, sobbing. "There was so much blood. It was all over me, and there was nothing I could do." Taking Enreal into my arms, I held her and let her cry. "I miss her so much."

Suddenly, on each one of Enreal's wrist's instead of scars were matching tattooed crosses, beautiful in color and definition. One had her name; the other had Valerie's name.

"Enreal, You are Christ. You will bring back all that is good and bring about the end of the Jinn. As for Valerie, Valerie lives inside you, and she will always be with you," I said, looking at her and holding her by the wrists. "These crosses are a promise from God. When heaven has been restored, you will once again be at Valerie's side."

"How do you know?"

"I've searched my feelings."

"That's funny, my father says that to me all the time—to search my feelings."

"He sounds like a wise man."

"He is that and more. You look so familiar and that raspy voice."

"You both must fight your demons to get your lives back," Tigist said, interrupting.

"Jensen," Tigist said, looking at me. "In that building behind you, you'll find the one who's taken possession of your body."

"Azrael."

"You must face him."

"Jensen . . . that's my father's name."

"No wonder he's so wise," I said, smiling.

"We'll walk with you as far as the building, but we mustn't enter. Our path is a different one."

"I understand."

As we walked through the wreckage of this wasteland called purgatory, we looked up seeing thousands of reapers circling around the building I was going to walk into. I couldn't help but think of what havoc Azrael has wreaked upon my family and those I loved. I still had his raspy voice when I talked. It was as if it would possibly stay with me forever.

"Jensen, this is as far as we go," Tigist said as we walked up to the doors of the building. "Walk through these doors. You may see awful things but pay them no attention. They're not real. Azrael will not give you up easily, but you will overcome him."

"May you find your path, Enreal," I said, looking her in the eyes, smiling before hugging her.

"Will I ever see you again?" Enreal asked.

"I'm sure we'll meet again," I said, smiling and shaking my head yes.

Taking a deep breath, I walked through the doors of the building. There standing in front of me in the lobby, I saw the ones I loved chained up, hanging from meat hooks. Written in blood on the floor was my angelic name—Spraygin.

"It's not real, Jensen," I said to myself.

"Ah, but it will be soon," a deep, raspy voice uttered.

"Come out from the shadows, coward!" I shouted to Azrael.

"Coward. You call us coward. You are me, I am you. We are coward," the creepy, raspy voice mocked. "Jensen, Spraygin, Jinn, angel, you are not who you think."

"Enough with the games. Come out from the shadows. I know that none of this is real."

"If you insist," the voice said, stepping out. There before my eyes stood the perfect mirror image of myself holding the Nevillin. "Do you not like what you see?"

"Azrael, this ends now!"

"It ends when I say it does."

"This is my life, Azrael. I'll be damned if I allow you to take it from me."

"It's my life now," Azrael said as he drove the Nevillin through my chest and backed away with the Nevillin still pierced through me. "Now it's over, Spraygin."

"You forget Jinn. This is my body. We play by my rules," I said as I smirked and pulled the Nevillin out from my chest. "You have no power here, the Nevillin answers to me, and me only." I said as Azrael became scared and backed away.

"You are nothing, Jensen, Spraygin, chaos," Azrael said, trying to conjure up anything he could to frighten me.

"I pity you, Azrael," I said as he backed further and further away from me.

"Save your pity," Azrael said as he lashed out and struck me with a barbed whip. "Pity is for the weak."

Catching the whip with my left hand, it wrapped around my entire arm all the way to my shoulder. As he pulled it, it tightened around my arm and began to sink into my skin. Taking the Nevillin, I cut the whip, and Azrael fell backward. However, before he hit the floor, I flew over to him and drove the Nevillin through him.

"Now it's over," I said as he vanished into a cloud of smoke and everything became dark.

Holy Relics

Jensen

Feeling the coldness of metal on my wrists, I slowly opened my eyes. I saw papers spread out on a wooden table in front of me. Looking around, I saw a bailiff and a woman sitting in a chair, typing. I was wearing an orange jumpsuit, standing before an empty podium where a judge would be. Looking behind me, I saw my mom, dad, and Octavia.

"Dad," I whispered.

"Jensen," Nathaniel replied, getting out of his seat. "What happened to your arm?"

"Jensen," Maya replied.

"Sir, I have to ask you to please have a seat," the bailiff said, walking over.

"Yeah, no problem," Nathaniel said, smiling.

"Thank you, sir," the bailiff said, nodding. "All rise for the honorable Judge Rouge."

"You may all be seated," Judge Rouge said as she took her seat at the podium. "Jensen Kane, your case has been heard by a jury of your peers. Do you have anything to say before sentencing?"

"I do, Your Honor," I said, remembering what happened to Juan Martinez. "My voice is raspy."

"It's been raspy since the day we met, Mr. Kane. Now if you wouldn't mind, do you have anything you would like to say?"

"Yes, Your Honor."

"You may rise."

"Ladies and gentlemen of the jury, I don't deserve forgiveness for what I've done . . ."

"I advise you, Mr. Kane, to watch what you're about to say in my courtroom. I will have you removed again if I need to."

"I understand, Your Honor, and I apologize for whatever I may have done or said earlier. Ladies and gentlemen of the jury, my actions were mine and mine alone. My only hope is that the jury didn't completely ignore the fact that Juan was a known affiliate and gang member of the San Juan Disciples. Your Honor, I don't deserve forgiveness, and I don't want it. My case is one of self-defense. Thank you."

"Mr. Kane, I appreciate how sincere you just were, but I'm not sure you believe what you just said. Through ninety percent of this court hearing, you've been arrogant, rude, and downright nasty with the words you've chosen to use. I've had you removed several times from my courtroom for your antics. With this said, Jensen Kane, you've been given the opportunity to be heard and show cause why judgment should not be imposed. This court has prepared a comprehensive sentencing order that is on file with the clerk. No legal cause has been shown to preclude the judgment and sentence. This case involves the completely senseless act of attempted murder on one Juan Martinez, a young man whom the defendant knew and attacked in self-defense. Jensen Kane, though self-defense has been taken into consideration, you are a very skilled and gifted martial artist, which makes you a deadly weapon because if provoked you can respond with deadly force. Therefore, Jensen Kane, you are found guilty for the crime of attempted murder on one Juan Martinez. For this crime, the court sentences you to serve a term of imprisonment at the Eastlake Juvenile Detention Center for no less than three years," the judge said as she hit the anvil. "Bailiff, take him into custody."

"Judge Rouge, his whole arm looks like he just had extensive tattoo work done," the bailiff said as he grabbed my right arm and looked carefully.

"And your point, Bailiff?" Judge Rouge responded.

"It wasn't there before."

"What're you talking about?" Judge Rouge said, walking over.

"This tattoo was not present when he was brought into the court."

"What is this, Mr. Kane?" the judge asked, looking at my arm curiously.

"A memento."

"Mr. Kane, no games. Where'd this come from?" the judge asked, looking at it closer, examining it. "Have you had this the whole time?" she than asked concerned.

"Yes," I hesitatingly said. "It's just infected, that's all."

"Bailiff, you may proceed," the judge said as the bailiff proceeded to take me to the back of the court.

"Mom, don't be upset," I said seeing her eyes fill with tears.

"We'll see you in the back, son," Nathaniel said as I nodded at him and the bailiff continued to walk me to the back of the courtroom.

When I looked at Octavia, she gave me an unforgettable smile and wink. When she did this, a great feeling came over me as if I was sheltered by love.

"For someone who just heard their sentencing, you sure don't seem to be shaken up about it," the bailiff said.

"What can I say, life's been good to me."

"And there's no way you had that tattoo already and I didn't see it. Who are you, boy?" the bailiff asked, placing me into a cell with the door open.

"I'm no one."

"You sure about that?" the bailiff said, staring at me as if he knew who I was. "Your parents will be back here in just a moment," he said as I turned around and saw a toilet and a small sink.

"Thank you, bailiff."

"Jensen," a soft voice whispered as I turned back around.

"Octavia," I replied hugging and kissing her, as Connor walked through the cell door behind her. "Connor . . . dude."

"No need for apologies, brother. I'm not made of glass," Connor said as he grabbed Octavia and I and pulled us together for a hug. "It's good to see you back to normal. Love the raspy voice and new tattoo," Connor said, patting me on the back.

"I'm so happy to see you," Octavia said, hugging me.

"Jensen," my mom and dad said, walking into the cell.

"Mom, I'm . . ."

"Say nothing, sweetheart. You did nothing wrong," my mom said, touching the side of my face before hugging me.

"Thank you all for loving me so unconditionally," I said, looking at them.

"Were just glad to have you back, son. Obviously it was no easy chore getting out of the situation you were put in," Nathaniel said, concerned and looking at my arm.

"Where have you been that you got this?"

"Purgatory," I said, "I confronted Azrael, he hit me with a barbed whip. When I caught it, it sank into my skin and tightened."

"It looks angry," Maya said.

"It's a gift," Nathaniel said admiring it.

"How could this possibly be a gift, Nathaniel?" Maya asked frustrated.

"Only a holy relic could leave such a mark."

"What does that mean?" Connor asked.

"This was the barbed whip they used on Christ during the crucifixion. It's called the Whip of Kismet."

"That would mean . . ." Maya said, looking at my arm.

"Azrael was the Sanhedrin guard who whipped Christ during the crucifixion," Nathaniel said.

"So what does all this mean?" I asked.

"I'm not sure."

"All right, visiting hours are over. I'm going to have to ask you all to leave," the bailiff said walking into the cell with the judge.

"She's a Jinn," I whispered to Octavia hugging her one last time.

"Who?" Octavia asked.

"The judge."

"How can you tell?"

"Trust me, babe," I said, whispering in her ear. "They were just leaving, Your Honor."

"Jensen?" Maya said, looking at me.

"Everything will be okay, Mom."

"Jensen is correct," Nathaniel said as he opened the door. "We were just leaving, Your Honor."

"Bailiff, you may excuse us."

"Yes, ma'am," the bailiff said, walking out the door behind Jensen's family.

"You ready to cut the shit now, Your Honor," I asked.

"Yes, why don't we, Mr. Kane? I know that's the Whip of Kismet in your possession."

"And?"

"The only way it would be in your possession is if you killed Azrael."

"You two know each other?"

"We were both Sanhedrin. I knew Azrael very well," the judge said. "Did you kill him?"

"Yes."

"You need to understand, he and I we're not alike."

"Could've fooled me."

"Mr. Kane, this isn't a joke. There are some of us who are just trying to live. There are few of us, but we have no animosity toward humans, or you," the judge said convincingly. "I was the Sanhedrin who stabbed Christ at the end of the crucifixion to ensure he was dead. I've lived with his death on my conscience for a long time. I never lifted a finger nor spoke out against any of my kind for what we were doing. The Jinn were created for one purpose and one purpose only. We were created to wreak havoc upon everything good and anything that was Godric's."

"You know the true name of God?"

"Godric Goodwater, yes."

"The dark lord is the only one that knows everything about Godric. As a Jinn, I always kept my feelings hidden, always living in fear that I would be met with death if any Jinn really knew how I felt. Seeing Christ hanging on that cross and watching the blood and water spill from where I had struck him, changed me, forever. I walked away from the life of being a Jinn. I embraced a human life, even fell in love with a human. Through that love, we had a son. He's part human, part Jinn. His name is Dean. He too is serving time at Eastlake."

"How do I know this isn't some trick?"

"It's no trick, Mr. Kane," the judge said, flicking her wrist.

There before my eyes appeared a beautiful spear. The end of the spear was golden with a piece of barbed wire infused into the blade. There was angelic script all over the blade and the staff.

"This is beautiful," I said, looking at the spear.

"It's called the Spear of Destiny. I've kept it safe throughout the generations. It's evolved from being old and rusty to being gold with the angelic script."

"You've kept it all this time?"

"I believe that it evolved as I got closer to who it needs to be passed to. I believe that person to be you."

"Why me?"

"There was a prophecy. It told of Christ walking the earth once more. In his return, he would rid the world of evil and recreate heaven."

"And you think this is me?"

"No, but in time you will deliver the spear to Christ," the judge said.

"How do you know?"

"I believe, Godric always said to trust in fate. This is me trusting in fate," the judge said handing me the spear.

When I took it from her with my right hand, it suddenly turned to fire. When I tried to drop it, I couldn't. In flashing scenes, almost like a movie, I watched as Christ held up a chalice and led his flock in prayer. I saw Christ's crucifixion. I saw him being whipped by Azrael with the Whip of Kismet. I saw two Sanhedrin guards laughing, making a crown of thorns before placing it on Christ's head and pushing it down. I watched as Judge Rouge stabbed him in the lung with the Spear of Destiny and blood and water ran out from the wound. The burning spear in my hand then turned to a bright blue light that moved up my arm. Suddenly, there was a flash of white light, and there on my arm appeared a cross with Christ looking out from it.

"Damn! That hurts," I said, grabbing my arm.

"It'll hurt for a while," the judge said. "It's time for you and I to part ways, Jensen. When you see Dean, can you tell him I love him very much?"

"You say that as if you'll never see him again."

"I won't. Jinn are already in motion to hunt me down and destroy me. The moment I passed the spear to you, it alerted every Jinn that the spear was in my possession and is now that much closer to reaching the chosen one. There's no doubt that I just signed my death warrant and marked myself for death."

"You'll be safe though. They don't know who I gave it to, all they know is that it's no longer in my possession."

"But they'll torture you."

"They say Christ sacrificed himself to save others. Now I get to do the same."

Marked For Death

Samantha Rouge

Sitting at my desk, I looked over Jensen Kane's case file one last time. Sipping a hot cup of coffee I'd poured just minutes before, I said to myself, "Boy, I hope I did the right thing." Taking a deep breath, I closed the case file and walked over to my filing cabinet. Coming from a window that was cracked open, I felt a soft cool breeze as I placed the file in the cabinet. In my mind, I had accepted my fate, but I wasn't frightened by what the other Jinn would do to me but I wondered if they would go as far as to exterminate my bloodline and kill Dean. But I knew that would be tough to do since I placed Jensen Kane in his path. My sixth sense was telling me that they would come for me soon, and I knew my time was limited. As I walked to my brand new Tesla model 3, I could hear nothing but the sound of my heels clacking against the pavement and echoing throughout the parking garage. When I pushed the button to unlock my car, I saw a beautiful owl land on the hood of my car.

"Where did you come from?" I said to the owl while looking around curiously.

"She's with me," a young lady said, walking up behind me. "Samantha Rouge?" she asked like she was confirming something she already knew.

Looking at the young lady, I found her beauty to be absolutely divine. She had long, gorgeous black hair tied into a ponytail and braided. Her skin was soft, white, and flawless. The sheath on her back housed what appeared to be a katana. All over the sheath were beautiful engravings of angelic script that looked like it was telling a story.

"I am she," I answered.

"You've been marked for death. The Jinn are coming for you, and you must survive. Your soul must flourish."

"Who are you?" I asked.

"Quiet, they're already here," the young lady said, looking all around the garage. "Tigist, fly ahead and show me what we're up against. Samantha, I need you to get in your car," the young girl said as the owl flew off and daggers came flying out of nowhere.

I watched as this beautiful young girl pulled out the most alluring katana. I watched as she hit the daggers out of the air slicing them in half with her katana. Suddenly from out of the darkness, I saw hundreds of Jinn surround my car and the girl.

"Danika, Danika, Danika. I've been looking for you everywhere," a hooded figure said in a female voice, walking out from in between the Jinn while Tigist flew overhead and landed on Danika's shoulder.

"You've been looking in the wrong places."

"I have, but now I find you here making the affairs of Jinn your business."

"Everything's my business. And right here, right now is my business," Danika said confident, and staying alert. "You need to learn your place."

"Look around, Danika," the hooded figure said, shaking her head. "I keep calling you that. What are you going by these days? Danika . . . Enreal? Not that it matters. With the snap of my fingers, my Jinn will attack, and you and that treasonous bitch will be no more," the hooded figure said as Danika looked around and smiled. "You're smiling, I see. You really think you can take us all?"

"I guess we're going to find out."

"I guess we will," the hooded figure calmly said as she flicked her wrist and a katana appeared, swinging it. Danika dodged it before blocking another feeble attempt and kicked the hooded figure backward hitting a whole lot of Jinn in the process, like a bowling ball hitting pins.

"Samantha, get in the car and get out of here!" Danika shouted as other Jinn began to attack her. "Now!"

When I started the car, I watched as Danika single-handedly engaged the Jinn. Left and right, I saw her mow through them as if they were a pile of dead leaves. There were Jinn everywhere. As I drove, I saw Danika jump on a black Kawasaki Ninja motorcycle that had been parked next to me. I watched her put her hands on the handlebar and took off. But how could she of done that with no keys? Continuing to fight the Jinn, she began following me on the motorcycle. Breaking through a security gate and flying out from the parking garage onto the main road, I looked in my side mirror on the passenger side. I saw a Jinn hanging on the side and one hanging on the back. The one hanging from the side broke through the window. Climbing in through the back window, it quickly tried to stab me with a knife, but I caught its arm. I slammed on the brake, and it flew out the front windshield and vanished into black smoke. The one that had been hanging on the back had flown through the back windshield and into the car. It immediately made an attempt to try to kill me as the car was spinning out of control.

"What's with the knives?" I said as it tried to stab me, and I caught its hand before the car stopped.

Struggling to get the knife from the Jinn, I elbowed it in the face several times till suddenly it was dragged out the back door of the car by its feet.

"Danika!" I shouted.

"Die, Christ bitch!" the Jinn shouted, grinning its teeth as it tried to stab Danika.

"Don't you know that's blasphemy?" Danika said as she wrestled to get the knife from the Jinn. "And blasphemy is punishable. . . by death."

After getting the knife from the Jinn, I watched as Danika straddled the Jinn and slowly buried the knife into its side.

"Go to hell, Christ bitch," the Jinn said with its last breath as it vanished.

"You first," Danika whispered in its ear.

"Leave the car, Samantha. Ride with me," Danika said, extending her hand out to me, helping me out of the car.

Getting on the bike with Danika, we sped off. When we pulled up into the garage of my house, I could see Troy was still at work.

"Why aren't you honest with yourself?" Danika asked.

"What are you talking about?" I responded.

"Embrace who you truly are, Samantha. Only then can you be free," Danika said, taking my hands into hers.

"I really don't know what your talking about?"

"When I come in contact with people, Jinn, Angels, you name it, I take in feelings from them. I even see secrets and no matter what you do to bury them deep I still see them. Be proud of who you are."

"I'm a Jinn. What's there to be proud of?"

"I've forgiven you. Believe me when I say I'm the only person that can truly forgive your sins. When you gave Jensen the Spear of Destiny, you embraced humanity, and in doing so, you became human. So you are Jinn no more."

"Troy should've never cast you aside."

"What?"

"I know that he forced you to do things you found repulsive," Danika said, looking at me. "I know you were forced into many sexual fantasies of his, and you went along with them just to quench his appetite," Danika said as I stood there, speechless. "Dean loves you Samantha, and there was nothing you could've done to prevent his addiction to Fazin. You need to forgive yourself."

"Who are you?"

"I don't look familiar?" Danika said, looking into my eyes. "Perhaps from your past? How about now?" Danika said as she moved her head closer so I could look deep into her eyes.

"It's you. How can that be," I said, rubbing my eyes in disbelief. "I watched you die on the cross. I am who delivered you to death's doorstep"

"You did. But I forgive you."

"I'm so sorry, for what I—"

"Don't be. You simply played your role. He knew his fate, and he paid it gladly. His sacrifice was only the beginning. His sacrifice saved millions. He brought many people back to the light."

"Why do you keep referring to yourself in past tense?"

"I'm Jesus's descendant. He lives through me."

"That would mean . . ."

"Yes, he has a bloodline."

"Is Jensen Kane part of that bloodline?"

"He played a part," she said thinking and taking a deep breath.

"You're from the future? Jensen Kane's your brother," I said assuming.

"From the future, yes. Jensen Kane my brother, no," Danika said, with a chuckle shaking her head.

"He's your father," I said shocked. "That would mean his girlfriend, Octavia is a decedent of Christ and she's your mother."

"Correct."

That doesn't make sense though. If you're the daughter of Jensen Kane, then you should be able to flick your wrist and hide your katana."

"Once upon a time, I was able to."

"Why can't you?"

"It's a long story," Danika said looking sad. "I've made a lot of mistakes."

"Is Dean there in the future?"

"Come with me and find out," Danika said, taking her katana out.

"What must I do?"

"All you have to do is touch the blade."

Suddenly from out of the darkness, a katana came swinging through the air at me, and Danika blocked it.

"Nathaniel, what are you doing?" Danika demanded.

"She's a Jinn, Danika, and worst of all, a Jinn that participated in the death of Christ."

"She's not like the rest," Danika firmly said. "It's important to the future that she lives."

"I can't agree with you on this. She knew Jensen was innocent, but still, she sent him away," Nathaniel said, taking more swings to hit Samantha.

"It was necessary, Nathaniel, and she did what she had to do to get Jensen and her son, Dean, together."

"Their friendship and bond is incredibly important to the future," Danika said, lowering her katana. "If you kill her, Dean will seek vengeance. This will cause a riff between them. You must'nt kill her," Danika said firmly.

"I hope you're right," Nathaniel said, lowering his katana.

"Oh, Princess, when are you going to learn? You can't prevent everything," a female voice said through the darkness.

"Still lurking in shadows I see," Danika said as a woman dressed in dark red walked out from the darkness. "Isn't that right, Rayne."

"Darkness is all I know, Princess."

"You must know this isn't smart, Rayne. I've forgiven you for the attack on me at the garage, but please don't press the issue. My forgiveness only runs so far. Even for you."

"That's cute, your forgiveness."

"What do you want?" Danika asked gazing at Rayne. "Did you bring your militants with you?"

"Their around. As for what I want, I'm just visiting you and Nathaniel, my family."

"Family?" Nathaniel said awkward.

"What's the real reason, Rayne?"

"Where's the parakeet?" Rayne asked as Tigist came flying down from the ceiling, landing on Danika's shoulder. "I've come with a message for you."

"And what might that message be?"

"You will hand Samantha Rouge over to us. Or you will die."

"That's the message,"Danika said smiling and mocking. "The whole thing, you're sure?"

"It's not wise to patronize me," Rayne said, flicking her wrist. "I just came to deliver that message. You have one day to hand her over. After that you will meet your end."

"Why not deliver me to death now? Why wait?"

"You know I asked that same thing and I was told "at the end of the day you're still family," Rayne said walking away into the darkness.

"What was that all about?" Nathaniel asked.

"Nothing."

"Nothing, Danika?"

"Leave it alone, Nathaniel."

"As you wish," Nathaniel shrugged.

"Danika, if what Rayne said is true, we must leave," Tigist said.

"What could she be plotting?" Danika, asked herself.

"Danika, what are you going to do?" I asked, concerned.

"Samantha, all you need to do is touch the blade, and you will leave with me." Danika said holding her katana out for me to touch.

"Thank you, Nathaniel," I said, looking at Nathaniel and smiling before touching the blade.

"You're welcome," Nathaniel said before I disappeared.

"Nathaniel, we must part ways again. But as always, I leave you with much love," Danika said, hugging Nathaniel before walking away into the darkness, disappearing.

Surviving Eastlake

Jensen Kane

The bus ride was long and rough. From the worn leather seats to the excessive wear on the rubber flooring, I could see the bus had seen many occupants in its day. Looking at the faces of the other boys on the bus, they all looked and reminded me of myself somehow as I could tell they too were misfits. I could only imagine the stories they could tell about how they came to be in the same situation I'm in. The shameful things they may have done, or even now, feel remorse for. I took the time on the bus ride to reflect on the tattoo of Christ looking up through a cross on my right arm, The Spear of Destiny. I wondered what role it would play in the future. When we arrived at Eastlake, we were escorted off the bus in a single file line and were told to stand at attention to meet Judith Fisher, the warden.

"Everyone, stand with your hands out in front of you and don't say a word," a correctional officer said aloud in a threatening tone.

"My name is Warden Judith Fisher. I'd like to be first to welcome you all to Eastlake. But before you get cozy in my facility, we need to come to an understanding. There are rules here, gentleman. I don't ask that you follow them. I demand you follow them. First off, I decide when you eat, when you shower, when you have visitors. You're new fish, and this is my ocean. The other boys here will try to hurt you, rob you, even rape you. It's important that you obey my rules. My rules could make the difference between your life and your death. When I find that my rules are broken, you will spend time reflecting on my rules in the brig. Some of you will get to know the brig well."

"Well, that sounds easy enough," one of the boys said, standing outside the bus.

"Who said that?" the warden demanded. "Who said that?" she repeated again firmly.

"That was me, ma'am," a boy responded.

"And who might you be?"

"Justin Asher, ma'am."

"Justin Asher, you were told not to speak nor move, and here you are flapping your lips."

"I'm sorry, ma'am."

"Not as sorry as you're gonna be," the warden said, shaking her head. "Take him to the brig," she said smiling at the correctional officer.

"Oh my god, please no!" Justin pleaded. "It was a mistake. It'll never happen again."

"Yes, Justin Asher. A mistake that I can guarantee won't happen again."

"Nooo!" Justin said, crying out while being dragged away.

"You. Who are you?" the warden asked, looking at me. "You have my permission to speak. Who are you?"

"Jensen Kane."

"Mr. Kane, I've heard of you. Attempted murder upon a San Jaun Disciple. I don't envy you. We have many disciples here. I personally think they're trash, and you would have done us all a favor by killing him. How do you feel about my rules? You have permission to speak freely."

"I think you're a lot of talk, Warden," I said as she smiled.

"Do you? Let me offer you some advice, Mr.Kane. Be careful the way you speak to me. It would be a shame for you to meet with an accident."

"Is that a threat?"

"It's a promise," the warden said biting her lower lip.

"Sounds exciting. I can hardly wait," I said, smirking at the warden.

"I think you and I, Mr. Kane, are gonna get along great," the warden said, looking me directly in the eyes. "Guards, take these boys out of my sight."

The smell inside the detention center was stale and old. I was given new clothes, white slip-on shoes, and three white jumpsuits. On the back of the jumpsuits stamped in black were the letters EJD (Eastlake Juvenile Detention). On the front left side were the numbers 72689.

I wasn't there more than an hour when I was met with hostility by the disciples. As I waited in line for dinner, I was approached by four of them.

"I was wondering when you guys would make your move," I smirked.

"You're gonna die soon, homeboy," one of them responded.

"Homeboy," I laughed. "Do any of you know English?"

"Fuck you!" one of them said, lunging into my face.

"Feeling froggy, bitch?" I said, smiling as I faintly whistled an old classic western tune.

"Sleep with one eye open tonight, faggot."

"Will do, ladies."

"Damn! That was tight. Are you sure you know what you're doing, pissing them off?" a kid asked, walking up behind me.

"I know exactly what I'm doing. Though I'm not quite sure what this crap is," I said, looking at the food on my plate.

"Ah, give it a chance. You might like it."

"Looks like something someone scraped off the bottom of their shoe." I said as a loud siren went off. "What's that?"

"Dinner's over."

"Thank God," I said dropping the plate of food in the trash.

The first night was the worst. While I was in my cell with only the dim moonlight, I felt like I was going to go mad. I could hear the whispers of other boys talking through their cells and the scratching noises against the walls that told me some of these boys were making weapons. Laying down on my cot, I was able to drowned out the noise by thinking of Octavia till I finally drifted off into a deep sleep.

As the days passed, the disciples ended their advances at me. I didn't know why since I could tell that many of them wanted to make an attempt. Those days then turned into weeks. This was when I had met Shannon Meccafee, a thirty-six-year-old woman assigned to me by the court to be my psychiatrist. I'm sure it was the adolescent in me, but I found her to be enticing. She had curves in all the right places, from her high heels to her beautiful light-brown hair. But what did it for me more than anything were the thigh-high black stockings she wore. Every now and then, I would catch a glimpse of her soft white skin up her skirt when she'd move just right in her chair as she sat across from me.

"Jensen, my name is Shannon Meccafee. I've been assigned to you by the court. Judge Harris said . . ."

"Wait, Judge Harris. Judge Rouge was in charge of my case?"

"No one has spoken to you yet?"

"No, why?"

"Judge Samantha Rouge cleared out her desk. Destroyed all her files, including yours, and disappeared."

"What?" I said shocked.

"No one knows where she went."

"So what happens now?"

"Judge Harris has gone through what little remains of your case, he has deemed it that if within eighteen months, we can prove that you are capable of joining the outside world again, you will be granted a pardon."

"Okay."

"This doesn't make you happy?"

"No, it does. I just wonder what happened to Samantha."

"Were the two of, close?"

"You could say that." I said rubbing my head. "So what do we do now?"

"We talk, Jensen."

"About what?"

"Whatever you want for starters, how's everything been since you arrived here?"

"Interesting."

"Interesting. How?"

"Over seventy percent of the boys in this place are San Juan Disciples, and they know who I am. They have a strong hold in here and everyone is scared of them. It won't be long till they come for me and the Warden, she uses them to strike fear into the boys here. There's also something illegal going on. I just can't put my finger on it."

"Wow, those are some serious accusations you're throwing out there," Shannon said awkward.

"They're not accusations. They're are facts."

When the disciples made their move, it came in the laundry rooms. Three of them came at me. All of them had weapons. One of them had a shank made from a toothbrush. Another had a thick chain, and the third had a broomstick carved into a point.

"Guys, give me a break," I said as that boy from the lunchroom walked in, interrupting.

"Wow. I picked the wrong time to walk in here. If you guys don't mind, I'll find my way out."

"Hell no, ese. Join us."

"I'd rather not."

"Nah, homie, we insist," they said, grabbing him and pushing him over next to me.

"I'm confused here. Do you just attract violence?" the boy asked me jokingly.

"It seems to know where I am most of the time," I said joking back.

"I can tell. Listen, guys. There's no reason for all this hostility," the boy said while one of them grabbed him by the collar. "Take your hand off me right now."

"Or else what, motherfucker?"

"You're a big boy. Figure it out."

"Damn, this one's got a mouth on him," one of them said as the one holding the boy by the collar let go.

"I'm sorry but was that some kind of gay reference," the boy responded.

My blood was beginning to boil. As every second passed, I grew more and more angry till I couldn't handle it anymore. I grabbed one of them by the throat and flicked my wrist. When the Nevillin appeared, they went ballistic and tried running away.

"What! Not feeling so big anymore? Where are you going?"

"You're not afraid of me?"

"Hell no, you're Jensen Kane. I know who and what you are."

"How?"

"I'm a Jinn. I'm not like the others. I'm what they call a half-breed."

"My name is Dean Rouge."

"I knew your mother," I said sadly. "I'm not sure if—"

"I already know. She's gone, she's okay, though."

"How do you know?" I asked curious.

"Enreal told me."

"How is it that you know Enreal?"

"She came to me in a dream. That's all you need to know," Dean answered wondering about my curiosity.

Angelic Blood

Jensen Kane

Nine months went by fast at Eastlake. Dean and I watched as many boys went missing every month. He and I became as close as brothers. The attack in the laundry rooms was not the last of the attempts made by the disciples to take Dean or I out. We constantly remained on guard, but it helped that I pulled the Nevillin on them constantly because they began to fear that I was a warlock or something worse. The warden became convinced that the disciples were completely mental when they began reporting the incidents to her. Through visits by my mother, she learned a great deal about Dean, I was given books, which I shared with him. My parents, being very generous, would apply money to my account at Eastlake to buy necessities from their store. When I told my mother about Dean having no funds in an account for the store, she opened another account for him to use.

It wasn't till the disciples began disappearing that Dean and I became concerned. Sounds of screams in the night and rumors of organ harvesting began to surface. It wasn't long after the rumors that guards came into my cell one night. I was injected with something that made me weak and made my blood feel like fire. I was taken to the showers, where my shirt was stripped off me, and I was handcuffed to the rusted exposed plumbing overhead. Left hanging there with only the moonlight shining through the windows, the warden walked in with what appeared to be a doctor. I stayed calm and alert still feeling the effects of whatever they injected me with.

"Oh, Jensen Kane. How I've enjoyed watching you grow the last nine months. You should be very proud of your body. It's quite a sight to see, and you've worked on it countless hours a day to achieve such masculinity," the warden said, running her fingers down my chest. "This must feel amazing to a seventeen-year-old boy such as yourself. What is this here? Looks like scarification," the warden asked as she grabbed a baton from one of the guards. "Tattoos," she said, biting her lower lip. "Do you enjoy pain, Mr. Kane?" the warden asked as she hit me in the stomach with the baton.

"I love it," I responded, looking at her and breathing hard from the hit I just took.

"The doctor here is going to draw some blood, and you're going to be good. Right?" the warden asked seductively, sliding her finger down my lips to my chin. "Right!" she repeated firmly.

"Sure. Why?"

"You have angelic blood, and that's worth something to me. See, I've found that there is a great deal of money to be made on the black market selling human organs. Just imagine the amount of money an angel's organs or blood would be worth."

"Angel's blood?"

"Don't play stupid with me. I know who you are. Angels have a healing ability, unlike anything humans have ever seen," the warden said as she took a knife and slowly cut her hand open. "Now watch and learn," she said, cutting my chest.

She quickly collected the blood from my chest with a small vial. I watched as she took the small vial and poured my blood over her wound. In amazement, I watched as her wound healed without a trace.

"How do you know this?"

"Let's just say I have my connections."

"You'll never get away with this."

"Ah, but that's the easy part. Your family will be told that their poor little Jensen Kane committed suicide after you accidentally killed your friend. When hearing about this most grievous act, they will break down in tears and ask no further questions."

"Well, you just got the perfect little operation going here, don't you?" I said and smirked.

"Don't patronize me, boy. We're both killers in our own rights," the warden said as the doctor finished taking my blood.

"Guards, uncuff him and take him back to his cell," she said coming really close to my face. "Goodnight, Mr. Kane," she said, walking out after the doctor.

As I sat in my cell, the blood in my veins began to flow fast from the rage building up inside me. I couldn't decide whether I should break out of this place now or wait. It would be so easy—flick my wrist, bust out of here, and kill the warden and anyone that would stand in my way. The information she knew about angels was dangerous. I felt that allowing her to live would be a mistake. Making a decision, I flicked my wrist, and when the Nevillin didn't appear, I was beside myself. I flicked my wrist over and over, but nothing. Why?

"What the hell!" I said aloud to myself.

"What did you think, Jensen? You can't call upon the Nevillin to do evil."

"Who's that?"

"It's me," a woman said, stepping out from the shadows.

"Enreal, what are you doing here?"

"Why would you go against everything you stand for to kill the warden?"

"She's dangerous."

"And you think killing her is the right thing to do?"

"How can it not be? She knows things about our kind she shouldn't know. She's killing humans indiscriminately to feed her own greed."

"Jensen, you're going to meet tons of humans you loathe, but we don't kill unjustly. You've become completely lost in this moment."

"Lost. I look around every day, and it would appear that all of humanity is lost, not me."

"Jensen, you're calling on the Nevillin to commit an unjustified act. It won't answer."

"But if it serves the greater good—"

"Do you hear yourself?"

"Oh, I hear myself, Enreal. Human beings are selfish and terrible to each other. They were given this beautiful planet, and they treat it like a toilet. They start wars with each other over money, then thousands of them are sent overseas to their deaths for their leaders' greed. Christianity and religion seem to be the ongoing joke to them. None of them know the first thing about any of it. This world is full of religious hypocrites saying you should live your life like this. You should live your life like that. You should read the Bible. You should go to church if you want to be granted access to heaven. None of them even know that it's all bullshit and it's gone. Many of them treat the Bible as nothing more than a made-up instruction manual."

"Do you not remember what you said to me? What you did for me?" Enreal said, showing me the crosses on her wrists. "You saved me from the dark place I was in. I would've never made it out of purgatory without you. You're so important to the future, you're better than this. I demand you remember who you are," Enreal said as she tightly held my hands and slowly vanished.

Suddenly the door to my cell cracked open as if something was guiding me or even tempting me to kill the warden. Looking out from my cell, I saw a guard. Creeping up on him, I silently put him in a headlock and waited till he was knocked out before I gently laid him on the floor. Looking down the long, dark hallway, I rubbed my eyes and sensed whatever they injected me with was beginning to where off.

"Please help me," I heard what sounded like a young female child calling out.

"Where are you?" I replied softly.

"Over here."

"How did you get here?" I asked, looking through the small barred window of the door.

"I'm not sure."

"I'm gonna get you out of here," I said as I flicked my wrist and the Nevillin appeared. I drove the Nevillin downward into the lock of the door.

"Oh, thank you so much."

"What's your name?"

"Danika," she answered sounding nervous.

"That's a very beautiful name. I'm Jensen," I said quietly. "How old are you?"

"Fourteen," she replied.

"Follow me."

Continuing down the dark moonlit corridor, we came upon an open door. The room was very well lit when I peeked around the corner. I could see what looked like the body of an eleven-year-old boy sprawled out on an operating table nude. From another door in the room, I watched as two doctors walked in, laughing, wearing scrubs.

"Look at this kid. He was so scared he pissed himself."

"Shit, what a nasty little piss-ant."

"Danika, listen to me. I have to go in there. You need to stay here and be quiet. Can you do that?"

"Yeah."

"Don't move till I come back."

"Jensen, what if you don't come back?"

"I'll come back. I promise," I told her as I flicked my wrist and my cross appeared and the tattoo on my wrist disappeared.

"How'd you do that?" Danika smiled.

"Magic," I smiled back. "Now, stay here."

"Who you got there?" one of the doctors in the room asked as I looked around the corner and saw that two guards were holding Dean, and he was unconscious.

"The warden said she wanted this one done tonight. His organs are to be removed and his blood drained. He's worth a lot of money."

"Is he an angel too?"

"No, he's what they call a Jinn," another one of the guards said as they dropped Dean and he fell to the floor.

"Fill this vial with the Jinn's blood."

"Why?"

"Have you ever taken a drink of a Jinn's blood?"

"No."

"You're missing out. There's no better drug in the world than Jinn blood."

"When do we get to carve the angel up?"

"You guys are sick," one of the guards said as they walked out the door.

"You," one of the guards sneered as I walked in the room, holding the Nevillin close. "You're the angel."

"He's beautiful," one of the doctors said, looking at me.

Blocking the guards attack, I stepped back, waiting for the opportunity to go in for the kill. The doctors ran out of the room, and the alarm to the entire facility began to sound. I began hearing gunshots, and when the guards got sidetracked by the gunshots, I pierced the Nevillin straight through their chests. Helping Dean to his feet, we ran out the door I had come in from, but Danika was nowhere to be seen. Looking down the corridor that was close by, I saw what appeared to be a SWAT team, and one of them was holding Danika by her ponytail. Flicking my wrist, the Nevillin disappeared.

"Dean, stay here," I said as I walked out into the corridor.

"Freeze!" one of them shouted. "Slowly put your hands behind your head and drop to your knees," he demanded as I quietly and slowly stayed attentive.

"Jensen," Danika said, scared.

"You're no SWAT team," I sneered.

"Let's just say we work for someone that is very interested in you, Mr. Kane," the guy who was holding Danika said as I looked at the badge on his arm, and it had three big, bold letters on it, BMA.

"How do you know my name?" I asked, surprised.

"I know lots of things, Mr. Kane," he said as I flicked my wrist.

Dropping Danika to the floor, another member of the BMA team engaged me. Blocking everything he threw at me, he tried really hard to hit me with the baton he was wielding. Flicking my wrist again, the Nevillin disappeared, and I caught the baton. Taking it from him, I hit him in the face with it. Without warning, Dean came up from behind one of the BMA guys and took him down with a steel pipe to the back of the head. Like lightning, I ran at three others, cutting the barrels off their guns. Taking them down fast, I turned around to see a girl dressed in black with her face covered. She suddenly flicked her wrist, and a katana appeared. When she swung at me, I blocked it. As our katanas met, she continued her fierce attack. There was no doubt that she was highly trained in martial arts and fencing. From out of nowhere, she threw a kick, making contact with my face. I fell to the ground.

"Don't lay another finger on him, Rayne," Enreal said firmly, appearing out of nowhere.

"She's so beautiful," Danika said smiling softly.

"I was wondering if you'd show up," Rayne said as she pointed her katana at Danika.

"Leave her be," Enreal demanded.

"Oh, I see you've got a soft spot for this little one. No doubt you and she have something very much in common. I wonder what would happen if I struck her down."

"Enough, Rayne, get the blade away from her . . . now!" Enreal shouted.

"As you wish, Your Highness," Rayne said as she swung her katana down at Danika only to be blocked by a spear. "Boy, I didn't see that coming," Rayne said as I jumped over Dean's shoulder and kicked her across the room.

"Obviously, you didn't see that coming either," I added. "How were you able to that?" I asked looking at Dean.

"I'm not sure."

"Jensen, get them out of here. I'll take it from here," Enreal said as Rayne got up off the ground.

"Where's the Elder Grimoire, Enreal? I know you stole it from the Hall of Shadows."

"Oh, Rayne, you have so much to learn. How can you steal that which rightfully belongs to you?" Enreal said as her and Rayne's katanas collided. "Jensen, stay steadfast and get yourselves to safety."

"Jensen, there's the main entry door down at the end of this hall," Dean said as we heard the sounds of katanas clanging together.

Around every corner, Eastlake had become a war zone, teenage boys were being slaughtered left and right. Making our way carefully to the door, four men stepped out in front of us with guns before we could make it to the door.

"Where do you think you're going?" one of the guards asked, pointing a gun at me.

"Listen, man, just walk away. You don't need to do this," Dean said trying to compromise as he flicked his wrist and the spear disappeared.

"Lie down on the ground and put your hands behind your heads."

"I don't think so," I said and glared.

Suddenly the man stepped back and began shooting. I swung the Nevillin every which way, blocking the bullets till I was right on top of all four of them. In one swoop, I chopped all their hands off where their hands met their guns.

"Jensen," Danika said as I turned around, "something's wrong." Danika whimpered and stumbled. Falling backward, Dean caught her.

"Danika, don't talk," Dean said, quietly holding her.

"How bad is it, Dean?" I asked.

"Look for yourself."

Opening up the corner of Danika's shirt, I saw a bullet wound on her stomach and an exit wound at her back. Remembering what the warden had told me about angelic blood having healing abilities, I went to cut my hand, and Danika stopped me.

"Jensen, I'm cold," Danika said as she began to cry.

"Jensen, she's in bad shape. We've gotta get her out of here."

Picking her up, we ran to the door and kicked it open. In front of us were BMA vehicles. Jumping in one that was still running, I held Danika in the back seat while Dean jumped in the driver seat, and we sped off.

"You're an angel, Jensen Kane."

"I am," I responded, flicking my wrist and cutting my hand on the blade of the Nevillin.

When the blood began to run out of my cut, I let it drip into Danika's wound. But it did nothing. Squeezing my hand tighter so more blood would flow out, I continued to watch as our blood combined, and nothing was happening.

"This isn't happening. Why the hell isn't this working?"

"You should have this back. You're gonna need it," Danika said, putting my cross in my hand and holding it there. "It's okay," Danika said as she closed her eyes.

Danika

Jensen Kane

When we pulled up in front of the emergency room, we quickly jumped out and took Danika into the hospital. Holding her in my arms, I could still feel a shallow but faint heartbeat.

"Somebody help us, please!" Dean shouted as we ran into the hospital.

"Oh my god! Get a gurney out here, now!" a nurse shouted to her colleagues as she ran toward us to help. "What happened to her?" the nurse asked frantically.

"She's been shot in the stomach. There's an exit wound on her back where the bullet came out," I said, talking to the nurse and lying Danika on the gurney. "Are you okay?" the nurse asked, seeing that my clothes were covered in blood.

"The blood is hers," I said quietly and concerned.

"What's her name?" the nurse asked before taking her to the back.

"Danika."

"You boys, have a seat. Where'd this happen?" a hospital security officer asked us as Dean and I watched Danika being taken on a gurney through double doors into the back of the ER, where we weren't allowed.

"Eastlake Detention Center," Dean answered.

"Are you two inmates?"

"How'd you guess?" I said irritated.

"I'm just trying to understand what happened, boys," the officer said calmly.

"I apologize. I'm just completely on edge right now," I said, rubbing my head. "Would it be okay if I made a phone call?"

"Sure," the officer said, handing me his cell phone. "How about you, son?" he asked Dean.

"That would be great, thank you."

After the officer set Dean up on a hospital phone to make his phone call, I watched as he went to the vending machine. While I was on the phone, explaining to Mom what happened, I watched as Dean shook his head in disappointment and hung up the phone. Walking back to where we had been sitting, I saw him have a seat and put his head in his hands.

"How'd everything go?" I asked Dean as I walked up to him after finishing my call.

"Well, let's put it this way, I don't have to worry about bickering parents anymore," Dean said jokingly.

"Did you get a hold of anyone?"

"My dad told me not to bother showing my face anywhere near him again. As far as he's concerned, my mom and I are a thing of the past and dead."

"I'm sorry," I said sadly. "Look at it this way. You still got me to kick around," I said, trying to lighten the mood as Dean sat there in deep thought.

After sitting and waiting for about a half hour, we were escorted to a room where we were met by a detective sitting at a table.

"Boys, have a seat," he said politely as we walked through the door. "Can I get you two anything?" he added leaning forward before having a seat.

"No, thank you," I responded.

"My name is detective Winters. You boys did a mighty brave thing at Eastlake, saving that young girl. We found that the warden at Eastlake was involved in money laundering and organ harvesting on the black market. In all that chaos and destruction, she was never recovered. Therefore, she is considered still at large," Detective Winters said, taking a deep breath. "Dean, Jensen, what we are trying to understand is how you were able to survive that massacre?"

"Why should we share anything with you, Detective?" Dean asked, not fully trusting.

"You know Detective what Dean and I are really wondering: how was Eastlake able to operate for so long and not be discovered?" I asked as Dean and I both stood up to walk out the door.

"You boys should know, if you're not willing to cooperate with us in our investigation on Eastlake, I'll be forced to tell the courts that you are both unstable to be amoung society, and they'll throw you right back into another detention center." Winters said convincingly.

"I hope they try, asshole!" Dean shouted, getting into Winters face as the door to the room opened.

"Dad!" I said, relieved to see Nathaniel.

"Detective, I'm Nathaniel Kane, and this is my boy's attorney, Pierce Hatchet," Nathaniel said, shaking Detective Winters hand. "Pierce, also represents Dean Rouge."

"You know, Detective Winters, one might question why you're questioning these boys without proper representation," Pierce said, informing him of our rights.

"Well, these boys were witnesses of a massacre, but they're not in any trouble . . . yet."

"You fucking asshole!" Dean shouted as he lunged at Detective Winters.

"Dean!" I shouted, getting his attention and holding him back. "I need a minute," I said to everyone in the room.

"Come on, kiddo. You feel froggy, jump again," Detective Winters said, egging Dean on. "I dare you."

"Get out," I said, looking over my shoulder at them and grinding my teeth at Winters. "It's not a request," I said as they all stepped into the hallway and shut the door. "I need you to trust me, Dean," I said, looking at him. "Pierce Hatchet is a great attorney. He's been working with my father for years. We need to trust him."

"All right," Dean said, calming down and taking a deep breath.

"Trust me," I said again, ensuring Dean and calling them back into the room. "You guys can come back in now. Thank you."

"Listen, boys, I apologize for coming unglued on you like I did. It was unprofessional of me, and I'm sorry," Detective Winters said, shaking Dean's hand.

"Now, Jensen, Dean, here's what we're going to do. You're going to tell Detective Winters everything you know about Eastlake. We are going to put your testimony on record," Peirce told us. "How do you guys feel about that?"

" If you think it's best, then were good with that," I said after looking to Dean for thoughts, and he nodded yes.

"Dad, this is Dean Rogue. Dean, this is my father, Nathaniel," I said, properly introducing them. "This is Pierce Hatchet, my father's attorney."

"I've heard a lot about you, Dean," Nathaniel said, shaking Dean's hand.

"Nothing bad, I hope," Dean said as Nathaniel smirked.

After going on record and explaining in detail everything that had occurred at Eastlake, we came to find out one of the men that had invaded the detention center was still alive but in a coma. We discovered he'd been taken to the Mission Viejo Hospital and was being held as John Doe. When everything wrapped up, Dean and Detective Winters shook hands and were cordial to each other.

"Thank you very much, boys, for your testimony. We'll talk soon."

"Detective," Nathaniel said, shaking his hand and opening the door for him.

"Jensen, you will be left in the custody of your father," Pierce said, getting up from the table. "As for you, Dean, we will make suitable arrangements for you tonight."

"Pierce, that won't be necessary. Dean will also be in my custody. Maya and I have already planned for his arrival."

"Dean, that's up to you," Pierce said, looking at Dean and closing his briefcase.

"Thank you, Nathaniel for your kindness. I've come to see that the apple hasn't fallen far from the tree," Dean said as he nodded and smiled at my father and glanced at me.

"What about our sentences?" I asked Pierce.

"With the testimony that you've provided on Eastlake and the fact that all the files have gone missing, I think it's safe to say they will look at your sentences as time served."

"Could we see Danika now?" I asked.

"That'd be fine. A doctor will be in shorty to escort you both," Pierce said shaking our hands and walking out the door.

"Jensen, Dean," a doctor said, coming into the room with a clipboard, only a few minutes after Pierce had left.

"How's Danika, sir?"

"She's alive, but due to the amount of blood loss, she's fallen into a coma," the doctor said, concerned. "We're holding her as Jane Doe until someone comes forward and claims her as their kin and shows us a birth certificate."

"Wait a second, no one has reported her missing?" Nathaniel asked.

"That's correct, sir," the doctor said as Nathaniel looked deep in thought.

"What's her name?"

"Danika, this was the name she used when she identified herself to your boys," the doctor said.

"You know something," Dean said, looking at Nathaniel.

"I might," Nathaniel said still looking deep in thought.

"Can we still see her?" I asked, brushing my father's thoughts off.

"You may. Follow me."

When I walked into the room where she was lying, it was cold and stale. Biting my lower lip, I thought, "Who is she?"

"Who do you think she is, Jensen?" Dean asked me as we stood there and looked at her.

"I'm not sure," I responded while I gave her a kiss on the forehead. "I'm sorry, Danika."

"Jensen, are you okay?" Nathaniel asked me.

"I feel it was no accident that she and I met."

"And it probably wasn't," Nathaniel said looking at her.

"Dad, do you know something?"

"No," Nathaniel said with a deep sigh.

"What was that?" I asked curious of the deep sigh.

"What was, what?" Nathaniel rebutted.

"Seriously, Dad if you know something, please share."

"I'm sorry son. I don't know who she is."

When we left the hospital and pulled up in front of the house, there in the driveway was a white four door Chevy Colorado with a red bow wrapped around it that said "Welcome home" on the front windshield while my mom, Octavia, and Connor stood next to it. Jumping out of the truck, I was embraced by all of them. My heart pounded with joy at the sight of Octavia.

"Hi, babe," she said as I looked at her and she gave me a little smile.

"I missed you most of all," I whispered as we kissed and hugged.

"Thanks, guys. I love it."

"We're just so happy to have you home, Jensen," Connor said.

"It's good to be home."

"You guys want to adopt me?" Dean said, looking at the truck and watching my family welcome me home.

"Everyone, this is Dean," I said, introducing him and watching my mother walk over to him and hug him.

"You are very welcome here. And welcome home, Dean," my mother said, hugging him and welcoming him into our home.

"Thank you," Dean smiled.

"I'm sure Jensen has clothes that will fit you until we get you some of your own," Maya said.

Walking into my room, everything was just as I left it. Throwing on a pair of jeans, I grabbed another pair for Dean and tossed them to him along with a Godsmack T-shirt.

"Thanks, bro," Dean said, catching the clothes I tossed him.

"Ah, shit Godsmack. I love Godsmack."

"You haven't heard or seen anything till you've seen them in concert. Hands down one of the greatest bands ever."

"Hey, did you write this stuff?" Dean asked, picking up a composition book with lyrics to songs I wrote.

"Yes, I did."

"This is some great stuff, man."

"I write at my best while listening to Godsmack," I said as Dean smiled.

Dean Rogue

Dean Rouge

Two weeks after we gave our testimony to Pierce Hatchet, the courts granted Jensen and I time served, and our sentences were exonerated. In that time, no one reported Danika missing, and her true identity continued to remain in question.

"You look deep in thought over there. What's going on?" I asked Jensen as we sat in Danika's hospital room.

"Who is she, Dean?" he asked, sitting there, looking at her. "This whole thing boggles my mind. Why would no one have reported her as a missing person yet? It doesn't make sense."

"Maybe it's not supposed to. Maybe she's not missing at all and she's right where she's supposed be," I said, taking a long sigh and stretching. "Just a thought, but what about that John Doe at the Mission Viejo Hospital?"

"What about him?"

"Maybe he's starting to come around. Maybe he's in less of a vegetative state by now and can talk."

"Yeah, but even then, he may not be able to talk. Maybe he won't talk to us."

"What if we were to shoot 'em up with Fazin?"

"I don't know. That's quite a stretch. I wouldn't know how to administer that shit. How would we even get it?"

"I thought you might ask," I said, pulling a vial of liquid Fazin out of my pocket.

"Where'd you get that?"

"Never mind that. What do you think?"

"No man, like I said I wouldn't even know how to administer it?"

"Haven't you ever wondered how I ended up in Eastlake?"

"Yeah, but I never wanted to pry into it. I always felt that if you wanted me to know, you'd tell me."

"I use to supply prescription drugs to a dealer named Rico Ramirez."

"How the hell were you able to get your hands on prescription drugs?" Jensen asked, interested in how this was possible.

"Well, let's just say I wasn't quiet about being a Jinn. Rico helped me tap into my ability to shapeshift. For some reason, he had a great knowledge of Jinn. In learning this ability, he had the idea for me to shapeshift into a nurse and go to different hospitals and steal prescription drugs. It became like a full-time job, and I made really good money. That was until I became addicted to it. Don't get high on your own supply."

"Do you have any idea how deadly Fazin is? I've heard people say it's worse than heroin."

"Yeah, I know more about it than I care to."

"Like what?"

"I know it's an opioid analgesic typically given to patients who are allergic to morphine. I remember reading on the bottle that it numbs pain. My mom, at the time, was going through so much with my father. He was constantly cheating on her with numerous different women. I knew with the powers I had I could do something, but I chose not to in fear that I could kill him if I were to lose control. I thought if I could just numb my own pain, it would make everything better. It didn't. I studied and found that Fazin happened to be seven to ten times stronger than morphine. At the hospital, I'd shapeshift into a nurse, and I'd roam the halls like anyone. I'd steal whatever prescription drugs I could, and the Fazin I'd keep for myself. It was stored in two-milligram vials. I learned to administer the Fazin to patients, and since physicians almost never ordered that strong a dose, it was really easy for me to administer a portion of the vial and pocket the rest so I'd have even more for myself. It was that easy. I'd hear every day of kids being yanked off the street for having a single rock of crack cocaine in their pocket. But not me. I was soaring by right under everyone's noses. I was a kid in a candy store. I saw other nurses who stole drugs too. They had no idea I was watching them while they would dispose of leftover narcotics. They're supposed to find an RN to witness the waste—meaning, you squirt it into a hazardous material bin while they'd watch. But working at the hospital, you can imagine how much people care about watching others throw something away. Nurses have roughly fifty million places to be at any given time, and about half those things involve saving someone's life, so any unexpected, tedious task is going to be rushed through as quickly as possible. Most of the time, I'd see the RN quickly punch their code into the machine, indicating that they'd witnessed the waste without actually watching the nurse do so. Not because they were irresponsible, although that'd be difficult to dispute. They just assumed the nurses were trustworthy."

"How did you get caught?"

"Well, one day, when I was high, I found myself in skid row. I remember not having any idea how I got there. I thought, how the hell am I going to get home? So I went and bought a car."

"Wait, that doesn't make sense."

"Going back to telling you how I made a ton of money, I bought a BMW . . . with cash."

"I can see how that'd of been a red flag."

"You were addicted to Fazin?"

"Unfortunately."

"And you're walking around with that shit in your pocket."

"Are you still addicted to it?"

"There are things that trigger me at times to want too. I've learned to fight them."

"Man, I'm sorry you had to go through that. Give me the Fazin to hold on to," Jensen said as I handed it to him. "Come with me."

"Where are we going?"

"Just follow me," he said, softly squeezing Danika's hand before we walked out the door.

"Okay, what're we doing?" I asked when we got out to the parking lot.

"Crush it," Jensen demanded as he set the vials of Fazin on the ground.

"What is this?" I asked awkwardly.

"Crush the vial."

"What about getting answers from the John Doe?"

"I have thought of another way. Crush it."

"No."

"Is it hard to get Fazin?" Jensen asked.

"Not for me."

"Then crush the vial. If my way doesn't work, then we'll just get another vial of Fazin and do this your way. Crush it," Jensen demanded.

"No!" I said, picking up the vial.

"You're still heavily addicted to this shit, aren't you?" Jensen asked, ripping the vial out of my hand.

"What are you talking about?" I said, getting angry. "Give me the vial, Jensen."

"Why do you need this crap?"

"I don't have to listen to this shit. I'm outta here," I said walking away.

"Hurt's to hear the truth, doesn't it?"

I turned around and came at Jensen like a monster swinging punches left and right. Each time he blocked or dodged them, it made me even angrier till, finally, I made contact with a roundhouse kick to his face. It was then that Jensen began to fight back.

"Dean, we're not doing this!" he pleaded.

"Oh, yes, we are," I said, determined.

Taking the vial out of his pocket, he threw it on the ground, shattering it. Just when we thought things couldn't get worse, we heard the sound of police cars coming.

"Dean, we have to get out of here," he said, slamming me up against the side of his truck. "Get in!"

"Go! Go! Go! Turn it on. Let's get out of here," I shouted, jumping into the truck.

"Turn off the vehicle and exit it slowly with your hands in the air," a police officer said over the intercom of his car as soon as we jumped in the truck.

"Officer, what seems to be the problem?" Jensen asked as soon as we were out of the truck.

"I'll ask the questions here," the officer said. "Now both of you, put your hands on the truck and don't move. We got a call that there was a fight in the parking lot. You boys know anything about that?"

"No, sir," Jensen said with a bloody nose.

"Yeah, we say no to violence, Officer," I added, smiling with a cut lip.

"What happen to your lip, son?" the officer asked.

"I bit it, " I said, trying not to laugh.

"You bit it?" the officer asked confirming.

"Yes, sir, while I was eating a sandwich."

"How about you?" he said, looking at me.

"Oh, my nose. I'm prone to nosebleeds, sir," Jensen said smirking.

"Is that a fact?" the officer asked confirming Jensen's statement.

"It is, sir," Jensen said as he and I busted up laughing.

"And what's so damn funny?"

"Nothing, sir," I replied, still laughing.

"Don't let this happen again, boys," the officer warned us.

"No, sir," we both said simultaneously as the officer walked back to his car.

"Sorry for kicking you, dude," I said apologizing.

"Ah, that's all right. I would've totally kicked your ass had the police not shown up."

"Sure, you keep telling yourself that."

"I'm just glad you didn't flick your wrist."

"I know this spear is cool, right?" I said flicking my wrist and the spear appeared.

"It almost looks like something is missing up top."

"How many times has the spear appeared to you?"

"All my life," I said as Jensen's phone rang.

The Sin Eater

Jensen Kane

Walking into the hospital, it smelt stale, like death. There was a cold eerie breeze gently flowing through the place. When we walked up to the information desk, we were met by a heavy-set black woman wearing a red dress underneath a blue jacket.

"Hello. Could you tell me where we could find the intensive care unit?" I asked her.

"You're in it. Is there a certain patient I can help you find?"

"Yes. I'm looking for a male Caucasian man, I would say he's in his mid-forties. He may have been checked in as John Doe."

"We have one male Caucasian John Doe, but there are strict orders here not to allow anyone access to his room. Only investigators and police officers."

"Why?"

"I'm not sure, it doesn't say."

"Okay, thank you," I said as Dean and I walked to the parking lot.

"I got this, Jensen. I'll shapeshift into a police officer and get us in there. There's just one thing, though."

"What's that?"

"Every time I've ever shapeshifted . . ." Dean said, pausing.

"What?"

"It's better if I just show you."

"All right," I said after taking a moment to think about it.

I watched as Dean gently closed his eyes, and in the blink of an eye, his facial features changed along with his clothes.

"Damn, you're a middle-aged woman," I said, biting my lower lip, trying not to laugh.

"I told you. This is humiliating."

"Hey, at least you're a hot middle-aged woman."

"Don't ever refer to me being hot again. That sounds weird, and it's not an exact science. But it'll do," he said, trying not to laugh.

"What should I call you . . . Officer Fine?" I said, busting up laughing. "You have really nice boobs, Officer Fine," I said as we both started laughing.

"I do, don't I?" Dean said, looking down his shirt and adjusting his boobs. "All right, let's get this done."

"Wait, you're gonna stay like that?"

"I can't shapeshift into anything else. No matter how badly I want to, I'm always a woman."

"Yeah, you are," I said, grinning.

"Shut up," Dean said as he started walking back over to the hospital entrance.

"So how do we get you in there?"

"Don't worry, just go in, and I'll figure something out," I said as Dean walked into the hospital.

"Hello, could you tell me if you have a John Doe admitted here?" Dean asked a different nurse from the one before.

"We have one, officer. If you give me your information, I can sign you in so you can go and see him."

"Mom, I don't want to wait in the car," I said, walking up to Dean.

"What are you doing?" Dean whispered.

"If I'm going to get an A on my class project, I should be able to go with you everywhere," I said to Dean. "Wouldn't you agree?" I said, looking at the tired nurse helping Dean.

"What is your project on?"

"My project is on 'a day in the life of my hero.' That being my mom, Nomi Fine. It's my senior class project," I said cheerfully.

"Well, that's wonderful. Let me just get your mom checked in, and I'll let you go back. But don't tell anyone I let you go back there, young man."

"My lips are zipped."

"So your name is Officer Nomi Fine. What's your badge number?" she asked looking at Dean.

"It's 72589."

"Well, that's great. I got you all checked in so you and your son can go back."

"Good luck on your class project," the nurse said talking to me.

"Thank you," I replied.

"John Doe is in room 303. Third floor. When you walk off the elevator, you're going to go left through the double doors."

"Thanks again," Dean said.

As we approached the elevator, a man dressed in all black walked up and stepped on the elevator with us. He was handsome with sandy-brown hair. He was tall—around six-one, maybe. I don't know what it was, but something about him struck me as odd, and he looked out of place. As he reached to push the button for the doors to close, I saw a small tattoo in the shape of a cross on his hand right above his thumb.

"Which floor are you on your way to?" he asked in a faint Australian accent as the door closed and he pushed floor 3.

"We're going to the same floor," I said.

"Intensive care?" he asked, looking at Dean.

"Are you checking out my goods, mister?" Dean asked in a female voice, looking at him.

"Why, no, ma'am. But if it wouldn't be too bold, you've gotta be the most beautiful woman I've ever seen," the man said as I held my breath, trying not to laugh.

"Why, sir, if I didn't know any better, I'd say you're hitting on me."

"Why, no, ma'am."

"You should be ashamed of yourself, hitting on me right in front of my son," Dean said, suddenly slapping the man in the face and then looking at me and squeezing my cheeks together. "I just love you so much, sweetie pie."

"You're freaking me out," I said awkwardly.

"I apologize, ma'am. Forgive me?"

"Well, I don't know," Dean said, playing hard to get.

"I didn't mean to offend you. Ask me for anything, and it's done."

"Oh, fifty bucks and an explanation for the cross tattoo there on your hand?"

"What!" the man said shocked.

"Fifty bucks and an explanation for the tattoo. You want me to forgive you, don't you?"

"All right," the man said, reaching in his pocket to get his wallet.

"I only have a hundred."

"That'll be just fine," Dean said snatching the hundred dollar bill out of his hand. "And the tattoo?"

"It's the symbol of the Vatican."

"Wow. You're far from home," Dean said.

"Well, this is our floor, Mom," I said.

"Again, I'm truly sorry to have offended you," the man said as we walked off the elevator.

"What's your name?" Dean asked.

"Lankester Keane, and yours?"

"Nomi Fine."

"And your son?" Lankester asked as the elevator began to ring from the doors being open too long.

"Take care, Lankester," Dean said as the door closed, and he didn't answer his question.

"He works for the Vatican?" I said, confused.

"What would someone from the Vatican be doing here?" Dean said in a female voice.

"I don't know. But he said he was going to the same floor but never got off," I said, confused. "We have to find room 303."

"Look, there's room 303, there."

"Why are you still talking like a woman?" I asked smirking.

"Sorry, I didn't realize I was still talking like that," he said as I laughed. "Shut up," he said shaking his head embarrassed.

When we walked into the room, we saw that there were two patients in there. Grabbing one of the charts off the bed, I read it, but this wasn't him.

"Jensen, I found him," Dean said, holding the chart from the other patient. "It says here he's in a coma, and he's listed as John Doe. Now what?"

"Stand by the door and make sure no one comes in."

I watched as Jensen gently felt the man's face and forehead. Softly he placed his hands on the man's face with his thumbs over his eyes. It only lasted a minute when Jensen abruptly let go of the man's face.

"This isn't him. This man was never at Eastlake."

"That was awesome. What did you just do?"

"Something my dad taught me a long time ago. It's called mind-jumping. All elders have the ability to be able to look into someone's mind if the person is sleeping or obviously comatose like our friend here. It's just very dangerous."

"That has to be him."

"What about this guy?" I said, walking over to the other bed.

"Yeah, but if this is him, that means someone switched the charts."

"We can't worry about that, right now."

Gently placing my hands on his face, I put my thumbs over his eyes. I began seeing terrible things—things from his past to things of the present. This man never contributed anything to society. He has always been a constant drain on the world. It was only when I heard him talking about the black market and organ harvesting that I knew I had the right guy. He kept speaking to a man with a deep Russian accent named Rashad Natas, whose face was distorted in the vision. The vision came in flashes. It was as if I was a fly on the wall.

"I asked for the kidneys of one particular boy. You and that bitch Judith better not be fucking with me," an extremely masculine black man said in a threatening tone.

"No one is doing anything of the sort, Rashad," Nikolai said cautiously.

"For your sake, I hope that's true, Nikolai, because if I think you just might be, well, use your imagination," Rashad said, as if he knew something more than what he was letting on.

"One more thing Nikolai," Rashad said handing Nikolai two individual pictures. "I want these two boys alive and unharmed."

"Is one of these two the angel you're searching for?"

"Perhaps."

"Rashad," Nikolai said with compassion before being interrupted by Rashad.

"If we don't find that boy I asked for, Agnes will die. And that Nikolai will be your fault."

"Rashad."

"Don't delay, Nikolai. You have work to do. Now go," Rashad said as Nikolai walked out of what looked like an office.

"Men, I have been instructed by Mr. Natas that we're going to bring the operations we have with Eastlake to an end. We're going there to annihilate and terminate everyone. No witnesses. Here's a picture of the two boys that are to be terminated on site no matter the cost," Nikolai told a group of men dressed as SWAT, holding individual pictures of Dean and I.

"Nikolai, what of Warden Judith Fisher?" a close friend of Nikolai named Mikyle asked.

"She's to be terminated on site."

Then coming in flashes, I saw Nikolai take aim. Seeing through his eyes, he had the warden in his sight. When I heard a gunshot ring out, a bullet struck the back of the warden's leg. She fell to the ground. I watched as Nikolai slowly walked up to her, reloading his weapon.

"Nikolai, why are you doing this?" she asked, looking up. "I did everything you and Rashad ever asked of me. The two boys are here."

"I'm sorry," he said, pouring gasoline all over her.

"Nikolai, don't do this," Judith pleaded.

"It's already done," he said, lighting a match, and watched as her body became engulfed in flames.

Then I heard another shot and felt a great amount of pain in my stomach. It was as if I had gotten shot. Nikolai looked down at his hands. They were covered in blood. Falling to his knees, he looked up to see it was Mikyle.

"Mikyle, why?" Nikolai asked, scared and shaking from the loss of blood.

"I know of your affair with Ava, and when the opportunity presented itself, I took it. I'm not the only you've betrayed either, Nikolai. Rashad knew of your plans to try and overthrow him and become the Sin Eater. I also know, he didn't sign the death warrant for the Warden. You were just eliminating a partner you didn't need anymore," Mikyle said pacing in front of Nikolai.

"I knew when you gave us the picture of the boys you were making your own plans. Tell me I'm wrong," Mikyle said, kneeling down and looking at Nikolai.

Nikolai, without wasting any time, pulled a knife and grabbed Mikyle by the throat and pulled him toward the knife, burying it into his chest and turning it.

"This was never about Rashad, Mikyle. This was all about your disgust that Ava could have loved me more than you. Now we will both die," Nikolai said as he fell backward, letting go of Mikyle with the knife still in his chest.

Opening my eyes, I shook my head and saw I was back in the hospital room.

"Wow, that was intense," I said after letting go of Nikolai.

"What did you see?" Dean asked.

"I have to get in there. Please move," a familiar male voice demanded from outside the door.

"That sounds like Lankester," Dean said.

"You need to let me in this room, ma'am," Lankester said from outside the door.

"And I told you, sir. No one is going into this room. Now leave before I call security and have you removed," a female voice said.

"Dean, we need to know what he's doing here."

"Okay, I'll take care of it."

"Dean, just get him in here, and I'll do the rest."

"Got it," Dean said, opening the door and stepping out.

"Lankester, I thought you couldn't make it. Oh well, you're here now."

"Nomi?" Lankester said, confused.

"You know this man, Officer?" the nurse asked looking at Dean.

"Yes, but I was unsure of whether he was going to make it. It's about time, Lankester," Dean said as he grabbed Lankester by the arm and pulled him into the room and closed the door, locking it.

Vatican Knight

Jensen Kane

Grabbing him and throwing him against the wall, I said, "Who the hell are you, Lankester?"

"I could ask you the same, kid," Lankester said, smacking my hands off him and pushing me.

"Who the hell are you, Lankester? The truth!" Dean demanded.

"Why do you have a deep voice, Nomi?" Lankester asked.

"Because my name isn't Nomi," Dean said as he shook his head and changed back into Dean again.

"Witchcraft," Lankester said aloud.

"I'm a Jinn," Dean said.

"What's the difference, evil is evil?"

"You know of the Jinn," I asked curiously.

"I'm a knight of the Vatican. It's my job to know of all supernatural evils and threats. I know the man lying there is a threat to the Vatican and all of humanity. I am also well versed on Godric Goodwater, elders, and the war in heaven."

"What did this man do to become such a threat, especially to the Vatican?" Dean asked.

"He's directly associated with a Sin Eater," Lankester said.

"What the hell's a Sin Eater?" I asked.

"That's a really long story."

"Well, enlighten us. We have plenty of time," I said. "Do you know who I am?" I said, flicking my wrist, and the Nevillin appeared.

"So the prophecy is true. You are Spraygin, Are you not?"

"I am."

"It was long ago. An Elder came. He went to Jesus's disciples and told them of what would come if people weren't called back to God. He told them that Christ would one day rise again and guide the faithful to the light. He would grant all who are blessed everlasting life in a new heaven that he would create. He would raise the dead and take them to his kingdom in the clouds. Jesus's disciples were the first of the Vatican knights. The elder poured knowledge into them and taught them the beauties of the world. He taught them different fencing and fighting styles to defend themselves if they ever needed to. Throughout the centuries, the elder went to specific individuals who carried with them the light of God. He'd whisper to them that they were in the grip of God's grace and gave them special duties to be carried out. He had them document the deeds in what is known today as the Holy Bible. As a knight of the Vatican, my duties are to protect the souls of the innocent and, above all, protect Vatican City and it's holy relics of our Lord and Savior, Jesus Christ. It wasn't long ago that the elder came back to us and told us about a great and terrible thing that had befallen heaven. He told us of the betrayal of an elder and the fight that was to come. It was then that we learned of the birth of a savior that would come and grant salvation to all the believers and restore heaven."

"Who was this elder? What was his name?" I asked, though I felt deep inside as if I already knew the answer.

"Nathaniel was his name," Lankester said.

"Very well," I said, taking a deep breath.

"I apologize if I upset you," Lankester said concerned. "I take it you know this elder."

"All too well."

"Do either of you know which of these two patients was the one that invaded Eastlake?"

"It was him, Lankester," Dean said, pointing at Nikolai.

"What are you doing?" I asked, grabbing Lankester by the arm as he walked over to Nikolai's bedside.

"I need to know for sure if this is the man who is in league with the Sin Eater."

"It's him. His name is Nikolai," I said, letting go of Lankester's arm.

"Where did you get that?" I said, looking at the knife that Lankester had attached to his belt.

"That is a beautiful knife," Dean added.

"Nathaniel gave it to my father a long time ago. It was a gift."

"So your father was a Vatican knight too?" I asked.

"No, he was part of a secret order whose job was to track, study, and perform exorcisms."

"Where is your father now?" Dean asked.

"Dead."

"How did he die?" I asked. "Was my father with him when he passed?"

"Your father?" Lankester asked, confused.

"Lankester, I'm Jensen Kane, son of Nathaniel."

"I ask you again, was my father with him when he died?"

"If you're the son of Nathaniel, then Maya is your mother?"

"You know Maya?" I asked, running my hands through my hair.

"How did your father pass, Lankester?" Dean asked.

"Well, he didn't really die. He disappeared, never to be seen or heard from again."

"What happened?" I asked, still thinking about everything I just heard.

"He took part in an exorcism that was well documented in the Elder Grimoire by Maya. Your mother was a well-renowned exorcist. She took part in more exorcisms and vanquished more Jinn demons than anyone in the order."

"The order?" Dean asked.

"The order that she built at the Vatican was a team of exorcists that were trained and devoted to her teachings of how to perform successful exorcisms."

"Were you ever part of her order?"

"Anyone seeking the title of a Vatican knight must become part of the order at some point and learn Maya's teachings. Maya's teachings have been passed through the generations."

"I feel as if I really don't know my parents at all."

"Should I continue telling you this?"

"Yeah, it's just there's much I didn't know," I said, rubbing my head. "There was a time when I became possessed and my mom acted baffled as if she didn't know what to do."

"It's because she didn't know what to do. My father once tracked a Jinn for weeks who had possessed a man who was already a terrible person. He would stalk women on the streets of Los Angeles, raping and killing innocent women. When the Jinn possessed this person, he did so knowing that he was an awful person already and wanted his soul for hell. My father tracked the Jinn to the Cecil Hotel in Los Angeles. The hotel was where the exorcism had taken place. This was the last exorcism my father ever took part in. My father turned to Maya for help, telling her that the strength of the Jinn was more powerful than anything he had ever encountered. When Maya and he exorcised the Jinn, the man lashed out at them, telling them that he had summoned the Jinn on the roof of the hotel and wanted the possession so it would make him stronger. He and the Jinn were very much one and the same, and he invited the wrath of the Jinn."

"Who was the man?" Dean asked.

"Richard Ramirez," Lankester responded.

"The Night Stalker," Dean said, shocked.

"I've read about him," I added.

"Yes, but what you read was not the truth."

"After exercising the Jinn, my father and Maya thought all was well. The Jinn possessed my father, and before Maya could do anything, the Jinn swore he would return and possess someone she loves dearly. He threatened that if she were to intervene ever again, he would tear her loved one apart from the inside out. This was the last time anyone ever saw my father."

"That's why she was scared and baffled," I said to myself. "Her hands were tied."

"Yes, if she would've done anything to help you, Rayzeal would've tormented you even more than he did and then killed you."

"How were you going to get the information you came here for?" I asked, handing Lankester his knife back.

"This knife was Nathaniel's. It was a gift to my father. Maya once told me that the knife will allow a human to see into the mind of another."

"It's one of the Trivium blades," I said.

"What the hell is a Trivium blade?" Dean asked very interested.

"It's one of the three nails that bound Christ to the cross."

"You mean, I've been walking around with a holy relic in my pocket?" Lankester asked.

"Yes."

That night, I couldn't sleep at all. I had tons of questions that I needed answers to, but I was unsure of how to ask. I also was in fear of what I was going to be told. When I walked downstairs that morning, I saw two police officers who looked calm and collected, speaking to my parents in the entryway of our home.

"Jensen, these two officers have some questions," Nathaniel said as I continued to walk downstairs.

"Apparently, the John Doe they took into custody from Eastlake was killed last night. They want to know if you or Dean know anything."

"How was he killed?" I asked.

"He was killed from an overdose of Fazin that was administered to him. The Fazin was not authorized by the doctor. We believe he was killed to cover something up."

"Do you know anything?" one officer asked.

"No, sir," I said, shaking my head at the officers.

"Listen here, Jensen, we already know you were at that hospital yesterday. We want to know why," one of the officers said politely.

"Sorry, guys, I can't help you. I was at lunch with my family," I said as one of them grabbed my arm. "Officer, I'm only gonna tell you this once. Get your hand off me now."

"All right, smart guy. If you want to play hardball, we can play hardball," he said, letting go of my arm.

"Officers, this conversation is over. Get out of our house," Nathaniel said, grabbing the other officer by the arm and showing him the door. "I won't ask again."

"You're gonna regret this, Nathaniel."

"I already regret letting you through the door," Nathaniel said. "If you want to question us again, bring a warrant."

"We'll be seeing you," one of the officers said, walking out as I smirked at him.

"Jensen, why were you at that hospital yesterday?" Nathaniel asked.

"I needed to find out who was behind this."

"And did you?"

"I did. What's a Sin Eater?" I casually asked.

"A Sin Eater," Nathaniel said, thinking, unsure how to answer. "Where did you hear of the Sin Eater?"

"I'm sure you already know how I got that information."

"You mind-jumped. I told you the dangers of mind jumping. If you get stuck in that person's mind, you could die," Nathaniel said as I looked into his eyes and saw the disappointment.

"I thought the Sin Eater would cease to exist after the fall of heaven," Maya said walking into the living room.

"Yes mom he still exists, but the information I got on the Sin Eater, I didn't get through a mind-jump but rather a Vatican Knight. And from what he told me, this Sin Eater has a very far reach into everything. Where did this guy come from?" I asked seeking the answers to my questions.

"The Sin Eater was a gateway that the dark one put into place. The Sin Eater's responsibility was to forgive the sins of the wicked. Once we'd receive the soul that he forgave, they would go back to their mischief ways in heaven and wreak havoc on its citizens. When the soul was captured and thrown into the abyss to seek counsel, the dark one would be able to transform them into what we know as the Jinn. There was a time when I sought counsel with God to advise him of the growing dangers of allowing so many unfaithful souls entry into heaven. I told him of the dangers of the abyss and harnessing that much evil in one place," Nathaniel said.

"Did you get the name of the Sin Eater?" Maya asked after taking a long sigh.

"Rashad Natas."

"Rashad Natas," Nathaniel said, thinking. "Where have I heard that name before?"

"Rashad Natas is the head of the Natas family. They are the wealthiest family in the world. They own the entire banking industry. The Natas family is said to be very powerful and has a very far reach over the entire world," Maya said, getting into the conversation.

"How is it that you know so much, Mom?"

"Some of us read," Maya said, chuckling.

"So . . . wait, you're telling us that the Sin Eater is Rashad Natas?" Nathaniel asked cracking his neck.

"That's exactly what I'm telling you."

"This makes him very hard to get to," Nathaniel said, thinking.

"Whatever we do, we're on our own," I said, beginning to walk back up the stairs.

"Maybe not," Maya said thinking.

"You said a Vatican Knight gave you the information on Rashad Natas?" Maya asked.

"Yeah," I said, taking a deep breath. "He was at the hospital to get answers."

"Was that Knight, Lankester Keane?" Maya asked.

"Yes. It was."

"Lankester," Nathaniel said and smiled. "I remember when he was just a boy."

"What did he tell you?" Maya asked.

"Everything," I responded.

Serenity

Jensen Kane

When I walked into my room, I saw Dean was still asleep. Putting on a pair of matte-black Beats headphones I had gotten for my birthday a couple of years ago, I pushed play on my phone and began listening to one of my favorite bands, Godsmack. Sitting at the desk in my room, I thought about Octavia. I could feel my hormones taking control of me as I thought of how beautiful she looked when I had seen her the other day when I took her out on a date. She was wearing a light-blue sundress that complemented her beautiful strawberry-blonde hair and blue eyes. She was so beautiful to look at, and her voice was so calming. I could tell that she and Connor both were still hitting the waves a lot by their tans. Full of thoughts on so many things I grabbed the composition notebook on my desk and pulled it toward me, I sat back and read a song I wrote a long time ago.

> **Jensen sings/metal sound:**
> I'm the nightmare in your head
> As you go to sleep in dread
> I'm the one they warned you about
> With a heart full of evil
> And a heart tainted by hell
> I will bring all of my kind down
> Let this be thy warning
> To all evildoers
> That I'm your nightmare

Jensen sings/metal sound/chorus:
A nightmare of disgust
A nightmare full of lust
A nightmare born of pure evil
I'm here, and I'm just the worst of
your nightmares
I'm the nightmare of lies
I'm the nightmare in disguise
I'm the one they prophesied
With a heart full of hate
And a heart full of lies
I will deceive all of my kind
'Cause I'm the nightmare that was
prophesied . . .

"Jensen," Octavia said, pushing the door of my room open, interrupting me as I was reading.

"Ah, shit, you startled me," I said, jumping. "Hey, babe?"

"Hey back," Octavia said, smiling and giving me a kiss. "Listen, Connor and I are going surfing and wanted you and Dean to come."

As Octavia stood there, waiting for my response, she thought to herself:

Look at this man, Jensen Kane. Prison time did his body good. He put on so much lean muscle. He looks great. I wonder if he has any idea of how much I love him. I love him for everything he is—everything he does and everything he wants to be. Still, I can't imagine what I'd ever do without him. He is my one and only.

"I don't know how to surf," Dean said, picking his head up from the pillow on his bed smiling.

"It's easy, Dean. You can hit the waves with me," Connor said, walking in my room.

When we arrived at the beach, it felt good to walk in the sand. It was warm and beautiful. The feel of the sand running up between my toes was that serenity I was looking for. Looking out at the ocean, all I could think about were the stories Mom and Dad told me about how God created all of this. It was blissful, looking out over all of it. It reminded me of why I fight the evil of this world.

"Why are you standing there all froze up?" Octavia said, laughing and smiling.

"I'm taking in all this sweet serenity," I smiled, taking a deep breath. "It's beautiful."

"Your friend Dean is no stranger to any of this I see," Octavia said as Dean and Connor were already out in the water.

"Dean, isn't a stranger to anything," I said taking off my shirt.

"When Azrael hit you with the Whip of Kismet and you caught it, did it hurt?" Octavia asked, looking at my arm.

"It did. It burned," I answered as she ran her fingers down my arm seductively.

"Let's surf over there so we can be alone."

"So what's the deal with those two?" Dean asked Connor, looking at Jensen and Octavia.

"Those two I believe were created for each other," Connor answered looking over at them, smiling. "You'll never find a better couple. Makes me kinda jealous at times just seeing what they have together. I want that."

"How long have you all known each other?"

"As long as I can remember. We all met at infancy."

"Holy hell! Well, aren't I just the third wheel?"

"We're in the same boat, my friend. Even when we were kids, it was always those two and then me. I've always been the third wheel. But . . . such is life."

"I really missed you, baby," Octavia said, smiling.

"I thought about you all the time," I responded, looking her in the eyes.

"What was it like at Eastlake?"

"It was hard. Day after day, constantly looking over your shoulder, never knowing what the day's going to bring. Everyone wanting to test you to see if you'll break. There was even corruption amongst the guards. I met Dean within my first couple days there. He and I formed a pact to watch each others back's till we got out. You knew I was sentenced to Eastlake purposely to help Dean, right?"

"You were purposly sentenced?"

"His mom was the judge that convicted me."

"Why?" Octavia asked awkwardly.

"Dean is addicted to Fazin," I said, explaining. "He was on a collision course of self-destruction. His mom convinced me the friendship we'd create would help him in more ways than one. He's also a Jinn, but he's unlike the others."

"I'm so sorry, you had to go through that."

"I'm not. It's made me a stronger person inside and out," I said, looking at her. "Do you know I love you, Octavia?"

"Do you know I love you, Jensen."

"I mean it," I said, looking her deep in the eyes. "I really . . . love you. I always have. I always will," I said, paddling my board over next to hers. "My only regret is that I never told you before."

"But you did. Through your actions. Every time you looked at me. All the times I needed a friend. Through all the gestures and sacrifices you made no matter the outcome. I love you, Jensen Kane. I always did. I always will," Octavia said before kissing me on the lips. "Now, I'll bet I can catch more waves than you."

"You're on."

Through all the waves caught that day and all the fun we had, the sun started to set, lighting the clouds into a beautiful pink-and-orange contrast.

"What are you looking at up there?" Dean asked as he saw me looking up at the sky.

"My sweet serenity, my friend," I answered, taking a deep breath. "My sweet serenity."

Casting all sorts of beautiful colors across the sky, I felt God's grace everywhere. While Octavia and I dried off, Connor and Dean walked off ahead. While Octavia and I slowly strolled up the hill, we walked down to get to the ocean.

"What's that?" I said as I heard the alarm on my truck sounding.

"Look at this shit," Dean said as he looked at a bunch of gang members sitting on the back of Jensen's truck. "Friends of yours?"

"I'll take care of this," I said, setting my surfboard down on a belt of green grass.

"What are we supposed to do, sit back while you have all the fun?" Octavia said, smiling.

"You know me, brother. I'm always down for a good scrap," Dean said when I looked at him.

"Back at it, are we? Do you just attract violence?" Connor said jokingly, looking at me.

"It pretty much knows where I am most of the time."

"We can see that," Octavia said smiling.

"Well, let's not keep your friends waiting. Should we say hello?" Dean asked looking at all of us.

"Definitely," Connor said.

The parking lot became dark as the sun set. The only light we had was a few streetlights. One at a time, the gang members jumped off my truck and began walking toward us as we walked toward them. We must have looked like a small army going to war. We all had set our boards on the belt of grass, except Dean.

"Can we help you guys?" I asked.

"We're here for that fucker," one of them said, pointing a knife at Dean. "Right there."

"Why?" I asked, confused.

"So you didn't tell your new friends here about all the bullshit you put our employer through," one of the thugs said.

"Employer. What the fuck. You're a bunch of dimwit thugs," Connor said with a chuckle, mocking them.

"You might want to put a cork in it, motherfucker!" one of them shouted.

"Damn, Dean. I can see you didn't have the most educated of friends," Octavia said, smiling and looking at Dean.

Suddenly with no words spoken, Dean took his board and hit two of the gang members across the face, knocking them to the ground. The other four then ran at Octavia, Connor, and I. As Connor and I took out the guys that came at us, we lost sight of the two that went after Octavia. As we ran to where we saw Dean standing, we gazed upon Octavia holding her ground against two of the thugs. Suddenly, Octavia threw a roundhouse kick that took one of them down, leaving only one still standing. The coward then came at her with a knife.

"I have to stop this!" I said, angry.

"No, brother. Watch this," Connor said, putting his hand on my shoulder, stopping me. "Besides, if you interfere, you'll just piss her off."

"Are you sure we shouldn't do something?" Dean said, worried.

"She'll be fine. She's not in any real danger, and if she was, the girl in black will come and stop it."

"The girl in black?" I asked.

"Yeah, she's saved Octavia before," Connor said, watching his sister closely.

"She has?"

"You know something funny?" Connor said, looking at Dean and I. "Do you remember when you and Octavia were attacked by Jinn?"

"Yeah, she almost died that day."

"Who almost died?" Octavia said, interrupting our conversation as soon as she pummeled her attacker and he fell to the ground. "You were worried, weren't you?" Octavia said, smiling and walking past me, sliding her finger seductively across my chin." Let's get out of here."

"I wasn't worried,"I said following her. "I was worried," I whispered shaking my head yes at Dean and Connor.

"We know," they answered simultaneously.

"Know what?" she asked.

"Nothing," we all answered simultaneously.

"She's a keeper, dude," Dean said, looking at me, impressed. "That girl can kick ass."

"Suggestion. Don't piss her off," Connor said, smiling and padding me on the chest.

"So what do you say I pick you up at eight tonight?" I said eagerly, catching up to Octavia.

"Eight. Let me think," Octavia said, biting her lower lip. "I think I'm busy."

"Busy?"

"Maybe," Octavia said as she kissed me passionately before we all hopped in the truck. "You'll just have to come by at eight and see."

"What?" I asked when I saw Dean grinning at me in the back seat.

"I think she likes you," Dean said.

"Shut up," I said as we all began to laugh.

Date with Destiny

Jensen Kane

When I looked at the clock, it said seven thirty. The time could not go by faster. My heart raced in excitement. I couldn't wait to take Octavia out and spend time with her. I wondered what she'd be wearing, and the scent that would intoxicate my senses. I wondered if she'd be wearing the diamond stud earrings I gave to her on our last date.

"I see you're taking Octavia out again," my mom said, fixing the collar of my shirt. "You're very smitten with her, Jensen."

"I am, Mom," I said, helping her fix my shirt. "I love her."

"I know you do. You have the same look on your face as your father did when . . ."

"Don't fill his mind with such nonsense," Nathaniel said, walking in my room inturupting.

"Nonsense? I speak nothing of the sort, and just like your father, your eyes give you away," my mom said, looking me in the eyes and smiled.

"Is it that obvious?" I said, looking at Dean as he tied his shoe.

"Kinda," Dean shrugged and smirked.

"You're no help" I said, shaking my head.

"Come on, man. I don't dare take your side over your mom's."

"Good answer, Dean," my mom said, congratulating him and looking at my father and I. "Take notes, you two. That's how you suck up."

"Suck up?" Dean said, confused.

"What would you call it?"

"See if I ever take your side again," Dean said, awkwardly.

"Watch it, kiddo," my mom replied to Dean and smiled, pulling us both toward her. "My boys, give me hugs and get out of here. It'll give me some time alone with your grumpy old man over there."

"Old. I'll have you know, my dear, like a fine wine I'm aging gracefully," Nathaniel said as he pulled my mom toward him and kissed her. "You boys have fun. I know we will."

"Gross," I said, looking at them embarrassed.

"I agree," Dean said, added with an unpleasent look on his face.

"Take notes, Jensen. This is how you get her to fall in love with you," Maya said as we walked out.

"Where did you learn to fight?" I casually asked as we hopped in the truck.

"I attended Asylum mixed martial arts. Why do you ask?" Dean answered.

"You're a pretty good fighter."

"Pretty good. Just a few minutes of fighting me and you'll know pain."

"How about you? Where'd you learn to fight?"

"My dad. He taught all of us."

"Nathaniel. Wow, behind the suit and tie, I would've never guessed."

"Honestly, the only one I've seen hold their own against him is my mom."

"Damn, mom throws down too?" Dean asked, shocked as we pulled up to Octavia's house. "I really envy you, man. Your parents, your friends, this is everything anybody would ever want."

"Well, they're all yours too, man."

"As far as I'm concerned, your parents are two of the most gifted and loving beings on the planet."

"They're going to ask you to be part of our family. By the time we get home later, you will have a room of your own in the house. But don't say anything that I told you."

"Why are you telling me this?"

"Because you have a tendency to be hard-headed."

"What are you trying to say? I wouldn't take the help if it was offered?"

"That's exactly what I'm saying."

"I resent that."

Dean was quite for the rest of the ride to Octavia and Connor's house. As we walked up the stone path leading to the front door, I could hear what sounded like loud metal music coming from the house, but I could not hear any singing, just an electric guitar and what sounded like a bass guitar.

"That sounds awesome," Dean said as I rang the doorbell. "I'm not hard-headed, you know. And I do appreciate you telling me," Dean added as I put my hand on his shoulder and smiled.

"We'll see," I said as Dean looked at me and shook his head.

"Jensen, how are you?" Mrs. Kryst asked in a soft voice, opening the door.

"I'm great," I said, giving her a hug and kiss on the cheek. "It's really nice to see you, Mrs. Kryst. This is my friend Dean."

"Hello, Dean. Where are my manners? You two should come in."

"Wow, you've all been busy," I said, walking into the living room, seeing Octavia playing a bass guitar and singing on a cardioid microphone and Connor playing an electric guitar. "I can't believe you guys broke this stuff out," I said, walking over to the synthesizer.

"Can you play that?" Dean asked curiously.

"He used to," Mrs. Kryst answered, looking at me. "Very well, I might add."

"Well, if memory serves me correctly, he used to play it beautifully."

"All three of you are amazingly gifted in the instruments you play, and there's no doubt they all could do it professionally," Mrs. Kryst said.

"Well, Jensen, you ready to go?" Octavia asked taking my hand.

"Octavia, you're not going to stay a while?" Mrs. Kryst asked looking at us.

"No, Mom, we'll be back in a couple of hours," Octavia said, as we walked to the door.

"Dean, you all good?" I asked.

Looking at the drum set they had, Dean said, "Yeah, man, you guys go have a good time."

When we pulled up to the restaurant, I couldn't take my eyes off Octavia. She was so beautiful to look at, and she wore the diamond stud earrings, but a different body splash that smelled just beautiful. She was wearing a gorgeous dark-purple sundress with black thigh-high stockings with black leather boots. Her strawberry-blonde hair and blue eyes did it for me. It didn't matter looking at her in the restaurant or on the beach, anywhere. I absolutely was head over heels in love with this girl.

"P.F. Changs. I love Chinese food," Octavia said, smiling as we pulled up to the restaurant.

"So do I," I replied, smiling back at her. "So I have to ask you a couple of questions?"

"What's that?"

"Connor was telling me about a girl in black that has helped you before."

"She's my guardian angel, Jensen," Octavia said, happy to talk about her. "I've only seen her a couple of times. The first time I saw her was that day at the ocean when you saved my life. She was standing behind you, and she told me—"

"That it wasn't your time," I said, interrupting Octavia mid-sentence.

"You heard her?"

"I did," I responded. "Her name is Enreal."

"Who is she?"

"She's a descendant of Jesus Christ."

"I knew she was a blessing," Octavia said happy. "I remember before she disappeared she told me she loved me and kissed me gently on the forehead. Being that she's a descendant of Christ. I wonder how she's related to my family?"

When Octavia and I were done eating, I took her for ice cream and a stroll through the Irvine Spectrum. I was so disappointed the night went by so fast.

"I had a lot of fun tonight," Octavia said, looking at me as I walked her up the stone path to the front door.

"Octavia, are you my girl?" I asked as I stopped and smiled at her, holding her hands ever so gently.

"I'll always be your girl," she replied, softly kissing me.

I pulled her toward me, hugging her. This would be the first time I ever took a long breath of her as I sank my nose down in between her neck and shoulder. Breathing her beauty in for just those couple seconds as we hugged I was as close to heaven that I ever imagined I could be.

Opening the front door, all we heard was loud music coming from the basement.

"Well, they're obviously still having fun. Come upstairs with me," Octavia said, gesturing and biting her lower lip. "Just make sure you're quiet, my parents are asleep."

As we went upstairs, she held my hand and led the way. Opening the door to her bedroom, she closed the door behind us. Pushing me down on her bed, she gently began kissing me. Running my fingers up her thighs, I stopped when I felt her G-string panties. As she stood up, I watched as she slowly began removing the spaghetti strap laces of her dress till it fell from her body onto the floor. Removing her underwear, she stood in front of me, fully nude and vulnerable.

"My God are you a sight to see. You have to be the most beautiful thing I've ever had the pleasure of looking at," I said softly kissing her stomach, working my way up to her perky breasts.

Biting my lip, I looked at her and laid her down on the bed. "I love you, Octavia."

"I love you, Jensen."

Embrace the Fate

Jensen Kane

The sun was bright and shining in through the window when we heard loud voices coming from the hallway.

"Oh my god, we fell asleep," Octavia said as someone knocked on her door.

"Octavia, are you in there?" her mom asked.

"It's my mom," Octavia said, panicked. "Yes, Mom," she answered in a panic.

"Open the door, please."

"Quick, get under the bed, now," she said quickly ushering me there.

"You have my shirt on," I said as she took it off and threw it to me.

"Hello, get under the bed."

"Sorry, I lost focus. You're so beautiful," I said, smiling and looking at her standing there naked. "I'm never gonna wash this shirt again," I said, putting it on.

"Shut up and get under the bed," Octavia said, putting a light-blue robe on and looking at the clock. "Mom, it's only eight o'clock," Octavia said, opening the door.

"I know Jensen's still here, Octavia," she said pushing the door open. "Do I look like I was born yesterday?"

"All right, Mrs. Kryst. I have no excuses. I can explain," I said getting out from under the bed holding a sheet to cover myself.

"This should be good," Mrs. Kryst said, looking at me disappointed. "Explain."

"I love your daughter," I said embarrassed.

"Oh well, that just makes everything better now, doesn't it?" She sarcastically smiled.

"It does?" I said, smiling.

"No," she stopped smiling. "What would your mother say, Jensen?"

"I don't know . . . congratulations?" I said, nervously smiling.

"You two downstairs now," she said, unamused.

"Okay, let me just find my pants," I said, accidentally dropping the sheet exposing myself.

"He doesn't have pants on," she said, turning and walking toward the door. "Octavia, he doesn't have pants on."

"I know, Mom," Octavia said awkwardly. "We'll be downstairs in just a minute."

"He's, um, wow," Mrs. Kryst said, turning and looking at me again.

"Mom," Octavia said, embarrassed. "Please."

"Yes, that's right. Um, you'll be down in just a minute. My god, he's beautiful."

"Mom, go away," Octavia said, pleading with her mom. "Oh my god, that was humiliating," Octavia said as she closed the door behind her mom.

"She has a point, you know."

"And what's that?"

"I am pretty gorgeous. That's why we're so awesome together. We define perfection," I said, grinning. "Our beauty cannot be duplicated."

"If we're so perfect, maybe we should do all that stuff last night over again," she said, looking at me smiling back. "As scientific research on our perfectness, it's only 8:06 a.m. We have time, and besides, my mom already knows you're here."

"Shall we?" I said, dropping my pants and taking her into my arms.

"Oh my god, so romantic," Octavia said as she smiled and laughed.

"That's me, baby. A regular Casanova," I said as we laughed.

"You guys think it's been long enough. We've been waiting awhile. It's cold now," Connor said as we walked into the dining room hand in hand.

"Sorry, we were doing scientific research," I said jokingly.

"Is that what you're calling it?" Dean asked, looking at us smiling.

"I hope you two at least used protection," Mrs. Kryst added.

"Oh my god, Mom, can we not discuss this right now?"

"You didn't, did you?"

"Mom, stop!"

"They did it," Dean said to Connor, chuckling.

"There's nothing funny about any of this, Dean," Mrs. Kryst said, and we stopped chuckling. "Wait till your father hears of this, Octavia."

"Don't be so dramatic, Mom."

"I guess you're right. He doesn't even have to know."

"No, he doesn't," Octavia said.

"Shit, he's never home anyway," Connor added.

"But what if you're pregnant?"

"Mom, you're being dramatic again," Octavia said as she hugged her mom and smiled.

"Jensen, are you going to tell your parents?"

"Tell them what?" I asked with a mouth full of food.

When we were done eating, we all went down in the basement where Dean and Connor moved all the instruments.

"Mom was okay with you putting all this down here?" Octavia asked, looking at Connor.

"Yeah, you know Mom and Dad, when it comes to music, anything goes."

"How long have all your parents been in business together?" Dean asked.

"A very long time," I said, walking over to the synthesizers. "When we were kids, we all had to learn to play instruments. I learned to play the synthesizer, piano, drums."

"How about you, Dean?" Octavia asked, looking at Dean.

"When I was in high school, I was in a band called Cruisin-N-Flyin. I played the drums," Dean replied.

"What do you play, Octavia?" Dean asked sitting down at the drums.

"I sing and can play the cello and violin."

"I told Connor about the songs you wrote," Dean said looking at me.

"Yeah, check it out. Dean and I were talking, and we thought, with Octavia singing, you on synthesizers and backup vocals, Dean on drums, and yours truly on guitar, we could become a band," Connor said, looking at me.

"Who will play bass guitar?" I asked curious.

"Already took care of that," Connor said when the doorbell rang.

"Damn Bear! What's up man?" I said, happy to see an old friend when the door opened.

"What's going on Jensen?" Bear asked in deep voice giving Jensen a hug.

"My God, Bear your still huge." "Bear, listen this is my friend . . ."

"No need for introductions here. We met last night. And Bear kicks ass on the bass," Dean said greeting Bear with a knod.

"You know something Dean. Dana Hills High School football team would've never been as dominant the years we were attending if it wasn't for, Bear."

"So the guys here tell me that your supplying the back up vocals."

"Oh no! No way! Backup vocals. Have you heard my raspy voice? I'll sound terrible singing."

"How do you know? Have you tried? We do metal. Your voice will be perfect because you'll sound scary," Dean said trying to convince me.

"Yeah, man, like Rob Zombie or Marilyn Manson," Bear said.

"Listen, metal, opera. Doesn't matter. I'm not singing."

"I don't know, Jensen. That raspy voice of yours could be pretty awesome," Octavia said, looking at me.

"I don't sing. Period. End of discussion."

"Fine. Dream crusher," Connor said, disappointed. "It'll have to be me then."

"Okay," I said, throwing my hands in the air. "I guess my voice will be better than hearing yours. You'll sound like a dying bird. Let me see the lyrics."

"I didn't write this. But it sounds really good."

"Glad you like it," Octavia said smiling.

"All right," I said, taking a deep breath adjusting the microphone over my synthesizer.

"Testing, testing," Octavia said, looking at us to make sure we were ready.

"Damn, a cardioid mic. I haven't seen one of those in a long time," Bear said looking at it.

"Best microphone ever. I will never use anything different," Octavia said, adjusting it.

"I remember in high school when you refused to sing at graduation without the cardioid mic," Bear said and laughed.

"The good old days. You guys ready?" She nodded. On three, one, two, three," she said into the microphone as Dean tapped his sticks together.

As we broke out into tune, we sounded great. We were all in sync. Octavia looked great, Connor played perfectly, Dean couldn't beat on those drums any better and now with Bear joining the team, I could only imagine we were going to become unstoppable.

Octavia sings/metal sound:
Through the trees
Let the spring time talk
About the times before man
Listen to the angels tell her tale
Let a guest come in, then walk out
Be the first to greet the mourn
The meadows of heaven, the great
harvest
The rocky cliffs the cold waters
untouched
The elks forest where the creatures
slept and see
Finally your number came up
Free your wings and fly away

Octavia sings/metal sound/chorus:
Come taste the wine
Taste the blood
It'll guide you to the light
So you're not riding lost til the end of time
Come surf the clouds
Embrace the light
It frees you from the walls of the dark
Meet me where the cliff meets the sea

Octavia sings/metal sound:
The answer to the riddle before your eyes
Is the dark leaves of earth are left behind
There is freedom in flying heavens skies
Turn in the sins and idealistic minds
And look to the garden scroll
Build a sand castle close to the shore
A house of cards from a Rolodex
Find hope in the fellowship that once was
Read from the scroll and only you will
understand

Octavia sings/metal sound/chorus:
Come taste the blood
Taste the wine
It'll guide you to the light
So your not riding lost til the end of time
Come surf the clouds
Embrace the light
It frees you from the walls of the dark
Meet me where the cliff meets the sea

Octavia sings/metal sound:
Riding hard like a shooting star
Come to life, open mind
Have a laugh at the orthodox
Come dig deep
Let the devil fancy
Come dance a jig at his funeral.

Octavia sings/metal sound/chorus:
Come taste the wine
Taste the blood
It'll guide you from the light
So you're not riding lost till the end of time
Come surf the clouds
Embrace the light
It frees you from the walls of the dark
Meet me where the cliff meets the sea
Come

"Holy shit, that was amazing," Bear and Dean said out loud as we stopped playing.

"We should give ourselves a name?" Connor said, pouring us drinks from his dad's bar in the basement. "A great band deserves a great name."

"I don't think Dad would like it if he saw you back there," Octavia said nervously.

"Is that what we are?" Dean replied. "A band."

"Hell yeah! We're family, we're a team, and now we're a band," Connor said enthusiastically.

"Just like that. We're a band," I said.

"Yeah. Why not?" Connor asked.

"You really shouldn't be behind Dad's bar," Octavia said nervously.

"The hell with being underage. We need to celebrate," Connor said as Octavia then smiled and shook her head.

"How about Embrace the Fate?" I said, putting my shot glass up to the team.

"Embrace the Fate," Dean said as his face lit up. "That's promising."

"Embrace the Fate," Octavia said, lifting her glass as Connor, Dean, and Bear joined.

"Embrace the Fate!" we all said together and toasted.

"Now how do we get the parents to sign us?" Octavia asked as we all looked at her.

To Live in the Light

Jensen Kane

After forming Embrace the Fate, Dean and I went to the hospital to visit Danika. It'd been two days since we last saw her and wanted to see if there'd been any progress. As we walked into her room, it was cold and empty, and on a bed where Danika used to lie, there was an old man hooked up to all kinds of machines.

"What the hell is this?" Dean asked, confused.

"I'm sure they moved her to a different room," I said, optimistic.

"Yeah, maybe she woke up," Dean said.

"Hello, could you tell me where they moved the Jane Doe who used to be in that room, please?" I asked, walking up to a tired nurse.

"I'm not sure how to tell you this," she yawned.

"What?" I said.

"I came in to change out her IV, and she was there. I turned my back for one moment to insert the new one, and she was gone. I can't explain it."

"That doesn't make any sense," Dean said.

"I agree. Could you tell me about what time this happened?"

"It was around eight forty-five, nine o'clock yesterday in the morning."

"Maybe she was an angel," I said a loud looking at Dean.

"What!" Dean and the nurse shouted simultaneously.

"I wonder if she knew, Enreal," I said.

"Thank you for your time," I said to the nurse politely. "Dean, let's go."

"Who's Enreal?" the nurse asked awkwardly.

"No one. Ah, thank you for your help," I said as Dean and I walked off. "She said yesterday morning."

"What about yesterday morning?" Dean said, hopping into the truck.

"You and Connor were downstairs."

"Yeah. And you and Octavia were upstairs having sex. What's your point?" Dean said, confused and wondering where the conversation was going.

"The only logical explanation is she's an angel."

"Yeah, because that's completely logical," Dean said condescendingly. "She sprouted wings and flew off," he added making fun.

"I don't expect you to understand, Dean."

"Well, shit, Jensen, you're not making any sense. Look, heaven fell. There's no more God, there's no more angels with the exception of your family. And unless it's been rebuilt, I don't think she's an angel, man."

***

After a couple of months' recording and finding what tone we'd become, it was at this time that we identified as a symphonic metal band. While attending a couple of college music classes, a professor said that I was one of the most gifted piano and synthesizer players he had ever met. Octavia discovered she had a set of vocal cords far beyond what she'd thought.

Her voice was beautiful and dramatic, even operatic. In one of the classes that Octavia, Dean, Connor, Bear, and I took together, we received a class project; and it was no doubt that we aced it. Our instructor was so impressed with our final project that we were asked to perform the halftime show for Saturday night's football game.

"What song are we going to do?" Dean asked, smiling nervously. "I can't believe the school is asking us to put on a halftime show."

"Guys, it's going to be okay. Jensen and I were ready for this. We already have the song we're going to do laid out," Octavia said, looking at Dean, Connor and Bear.

"How would you two have known to be ready for something like this?" Bear asked.

"Well, Professor Schulz is the one in charge of putting together the halftime show for the football game, and we thought to ourselves, let's try and get Embrace the Fate on the line-up," I said in a convincing tone.

"We even made copies for all of you to read and approve," Octavia said as she walked over to them and handed them a copy.

"Wow, this is really good, Octavia," Connor said smiling.

"I know Jensen wrote the lyrics. Did you write the music too?" Dean said, looking at me.

"I did."

"This is amazing," Bear said.

"We know. I'm glad you like it," I said.

"Dude, I love it. The way this will open with the synthesizer is going to be wicked," Dean said excited.

***

It wasn't long before the big day was here. We were all really nervous. As we walked up onto the stage, the crowd in the bleachers went wild. My synthesizer looked awesome; it was like I was up on my own little high-rise. My synthesizer had long wide metal wind pipes that looked worn, sticking out all over the sides. My palms were clammy. Looking out at the crowd, I saw people in the bleachers and people standing beside the bleachers. There were circles of people in common areas all around the field, standing and waiting. The place was packed full as if they all came just to see us. Adjusting my microphone, I placed my fingers on the keys and began playing softly. Looking out, I saw my parents and Octavia walking through the crowd. I watched as I saw five people get up from their seats in the front row just for them to have a seat. When Octavia walked up onto the stage, the crowd went ballistic, screaming, cheering, shouting her name. It was the most amazing thing I'd ever seen, and it gave me a rush.

"How are you all doing tonight?" Octavia said to the crowd as she adjusted her microphone, and I still played softly in the background. "So we thought we'd come to see all you amazing people tonight and give you a show. How about that?" she said as the crowd continued to cheer. "The song you're about to hear is called 'I am the Story."

Octavia sings/metal sound:
'Twas the night before
A battle for the world
No words, just demons crying
I rode the wildfire
'Twas a blazing pyre
Now that our worlds collide
You think you found the answer
For I am the necromancer
Forget the poetry
The cancer's in the world
Now we're living in desperate times

Octavia sings/metal sound/chorus:
I've got the voice that will never fade
I've got the dreams and innocence of
every man
You'll see me soaring across the blue,
blue sky
You'll dream of me beneath the moonlit
sky
I've got the story that you need to read
I am the memory that you hold deep

Octavia sings/metal sound
Returning from that journey
An unknown destination
I'm the tale they've read to you
When it starts the night
I'll battle the Jinn and hellfire
I'll banish them to the depths of hell
A man's imagination
It's a dream emporium
Just think of all the tales they've read you
It's the story you can't escape
While you intoxicate
The cold thought of just living in desperate times

Octavia sings/metal sound/chorus:
I've got the voice that will never fade
I am the dreams and innocence of every man
You'll see me soaring across the blue, blue sky
You'll dream of me beneath the moonlit sky
I've become the story that you need to read
I've become every memory that you hold deep

Octavia sings operatic/instrumental sound
Forever
The voice
That will never fade
Innocence
Of this world
Dream of me
Innocence
Of this world

Octavia sings/metal sound/chorus:
I've got the voice that will never fade
With the dreams and innocence of every man
You see me soar through blue, blue sky
Breaking through your moonlit sky
I am the story that you need to read
I am the memory that you hold deep
[*Repeat chorus while song fades out*]

"Thank you," Octavia said to the crowd as the lights dimmed. "Okay, so we're going to slow it down a little with a song called 'Dream of Me.'"

Octavia sings softly/instrumental sound:
Forever float away with me
Just once is all I need
Try not to fall in love with me
Forever float away with me
My love, it lies so deep
You'll always want to dream of me

Octavia sings/metal sound:
Would you do this for me
Fly through the sky and change the stars
Would you do it for me
Turn loose the heavens within
I'll take you away
On that lonely day
Just the thought of you and I
Puts us in heaven's grace

Octavia sings/metal sound/chorus:
Forever float away with me
Just once is all I need
Try not to fall in love with me
Forever float away with me
My love, it lies so deep
You'll forever want to dream of me

Jensen sings operatic/metal sound:
Dream of her . . . oh . . .

Octavia sings operatic/metal sound:
Come out, come out wherever you are
So lost in this sleep
Give in, give in to my touch
And get a good taste for my lust
Here your task is to dream of me
But are you sure you're asleep

Octavia sings/metal sound/chorus:
Forever float away with me
Just once is all I need
Try not to fall in love with me
Forever float away with me
My love, it lies so deep
Now and for eternity you'll forever
dream of me

Jensen sings operatic/metal sound:
Dream of her . . . yeah . . . yeah . . .

Octavia sings softly/instrumental sound:
Forever float away with me
Now once and for all, is what I need
You'll now fall in love with me
Forever float away with me
Your love, it lies beneath
It now belongs to me

Jensen sings operatic/metal sound
Dream of her . . . yeah . . .

[Song fades out/ending]

"Guys, that was incredible!" Bear said excited.

We said goodnight to the crowd and thanked them for coming out.

"So this is what it's like to live in the light. I could get used to this," Dean said smiling.

"What an adrenaline rush. It's really too bad we were only set to do the two songs," Connor said.

"Well, living in the light guys, you should get used to it. You're now under contract with Nuclear Bullet," Nathaniel said, walking up, putting his hands on our shoulders.

"I'm so proud of all of you," Nathaniel said smiling.

"Mom, Dad," Octavia said as her parents walked up to her and Connor.

"We're so proud of you both."

"Listen to that crowd out there. They are no longer interested in the football game. They would rather have you guys play to them all night. That kind of talent doesn't just happen," Octavia's dad said, making us all listen.

"Guys, you need to check this out. Our performance just went viral. Someone must've been recording and put it on YouTube. We're at 318K views," Dean said.

"Guys, I don't think I can handle this," Bear said holding his head in his hand. "Ahhhhh!!!!!!" Bear shouted in excitement.

"That's for the history books. I don't think any band has ever gotten that many views in fifteen minutes of being posted," Connor said.

"Is that even possible?" I said, looking at the screen of the iPhone Dean had.

"You can't be reading that right," Octavia's mother said.

"I am reading it right, I'm looking at it right now, and I'm telling you it's at 333K now."

The Secret

Jensen Kane

It didn't take long to complete our debut album. Octavia and I had written all the music in advance as soon as we were signed to Nuclear Bullet. We all spent countless hours in the recording studio. I always thought that it would be super easy to be a musician. How wrong I was. It's truly hard work and sacrifice. But nevertheless, we completed our debut album on time and were hyping ourselves up for our first tour. We had two singles that hit number one for five weeks in a row. After much thought and discussion, we all decided that we would kick off our tour by going to Saudi Arabia and playing for our American soldiers.

"You know, kids, we need to discuss starting your tour off in Saudi Arabia," Nathaniel said, walking into the recording studio of Nuclear Bullet records. "It's not a good idea."

"What's there to discuss?" Dean asked.

"There are a lot of dangers there that we don't think you guys have taken into consideration," Maya said, looking at Dean and I.

"Mom, we've discussed it, and we're doing this. We know the risks. We know the problems with ISIS and other terrorist groups, but we can handle ourselves," I said understanding their concern.

"What you fail to understand is that ninety percent of ISIS and these other militant groups are Jinn," Nathaniel said genuinely concerned. "The Middle East is swarming with 'em. This will put you all at very high risk."

"Look, we understand your concerns, but we've got to do this. It will be a good way for us to show our support for our soldiers, and it's a risk we are willing to take," Octavia said.

"We understand, we all must stay steadfast and mindful," Nathaniel said after taking a deep breath.

"We all?" Connor asked. "Are you guys coming with us?"

"Yes, Nathaniel and I will be accompanying you," Maya said.

***

The day was here. As we boarded the plane, Octavia and I were super nervous. I couldn't let go of what Nathaniel had said about the Middle East and the Jinn.

"Sitting in first class, ah, yeah, we should never ride coach again," Connor said, taking a seat next to Dean.

"We'll have to get used to a lot of things. The laps of luxury, baby," Bear said, laughing.

After a thirteen-hour flight, we landed in Jeddah, Saudi Arabia. The airport we landed at was King Abdulaziz International. It was nothing like I thought it would be. It was beautiful. Everywhere I looked, I saw happy people and the airport was very luxurious. We were greeted by an overly nice man named Abir.

"Welcome to Saudi Arabia," Abir said, smiling with a sign in his hand that said Embrace the Fate. "You guys stick out like a sore thumb between the tattoos and piercings."

"Were we that obvious?" Octavia said, chuckling with a smile.

"Any good places to pick up something to eat, Abir?" Nathaniel asked.

"Oh, yes, sir. Let's get you all in the limo, and we'll stop and get you something on the way to the hotel," Abir said, grabbing our bags and putting them in the trunk. "Are you guys still staying at the Abraj Kudai Hotel?"

"Yes," Connor responded.

"You know the Abraj Kudai Hotel just became the world's largest hotel," Abir said, politely making conversation.

"That's cool," Dean mumbled.

"Those are very beautiful earrings you have there, young lady," Abir said, looking at Octavia.

"Well, thank you, Abir."

"A very special someone, I sense, gave those to you," Abir added still looking at Octavia.

"Yes," Octavia said as she grabbed my hand and squeezed it passionately.

When we pulled up to the hotel, it was gorgeous. It was desert tan with light emerald green on the outside. The lobby was beautiful with huge crystal chandeliers and marble flooring. It was decked out with gold trimming everywhere. As we walked through the lobby, a woman wearing a turban with her face covered bumped into Octavia.

"Excuse me," Octavia said politely.

"You carry something very special there, the blessing," the lady said and smiled, turning around. "It'll be very important to the future. The world will be blessed on the day of its birth," she said, putting her hand on Octavia's stomach before walking away.

"Gee, I wonder what that was about?" Bear said.

"Wait, you didn't understand her?" Octavia asked, confused.

"Um, I don't speak Arabic, and neither do you," Connor said.

"What are you talking about? She spoke in clear English."

"Okay, someone needs caffeine."

"Nathaniel, what do you think of Abir?" Maya asked.

"I don't like him. I don't like us even being here. I feel danger is all around us."

"Nathaniel, you're paranoid."

"Abir has a very high interest in Octavia and Jensen both. And it's not the starstruck-fan interest. It's something much more elusive."

***

After we were checked into our rooms and evening came, we were due to appear at a press conference where interviewers from Saudi Arabia and America both could ask questions and get answers. As we walked into the press room, I saw a huge poster of us on the wall. In front of the poster was a long table with chairs where we would sit and answer questions.

Immediately after we sat down, the conference started, and interviewers and journalists alike began asking their questions.

"Jensen Kane, are you and Embrace the Fate nervous about this being your first real concert?" a slender American journalist asked

"No," I said, shaking my head.

"Why is that?" a bearded dark man wearing a keffiyeh asked.

"Because this isn't our first real concert. This is our first real tour, and we're excited, not nervous."

"Octavia, why would you guys start your world tour here in Saudi Arabia at the King Fahd Cultural Centre?" a young American women asked.

"Why not?" Octavia shrugged. "The King Fahd Cultural Centre was pleased to host our troops, and we're honored to play there."

"Do you have anything to say to your fans as they question the meaning behind your lyrics?" another journalist asked.

"The meaning behind our lyrics?" Octavia responded, shrugging. "I'm not sure I understand your question."

"Some of your fans have been outspoken about your lyrics. They say you're singing about a prophesied antichrist."

"No comment," Octavia said, shaking her head. "Next question, please."

"Why are you avoiding the question, Octavia?"

"Listen, if people want to read into our lyrics or question what we're singing about, that's their right, and who are we to stop them?"

"Yes, but are the rumors true?"

"What do you think?" Octavia said, shaking her head. "Next question."

"Is it true you've all received death threats for being here in Saudi Arabia?"

"That's untrue," Dean said. "Even if there were threats, that's all they'd be."

"Octavia, are you okay? Where are you going?" I asked as she, all of a sudden, got up and walked off-stage not answering me.

Connor, Dean, and I stayed for the questions as I watched Octavia pursue the woman who had badgered her about the meaning of our lyrics.

"Ma'am, who are you?" Octavia shouted at the woman. "Ma'am, I'm talking to you."

"It's not safe for you here. You should go back to your country," the woman said, turning around but wasn't the same woman with the questions.

"What do you mean it's not safe here?" Octavia asked, confused. "And what are you?"

"You really don't know what you're carrying there, do you? It will be the blessing that Godric's earth has needed for a long time. Take this and find the truth for yourself, Octavia," the woman said, handing her a pregnancy test and gently touching her stomach.

"Who are you, please? I must know."

"My name is Athena Goodwater," the woman answered before turning and vanishing.

Walking back to the press conference Octavia looked at the pregnancy test and couldn't help but wonder if it could be true. Walking in Jensen made eye contact with her and he could tell by the look on her face she was done answering questions.

"Listen, everyone. We love and appreciate that you've all come here to join us in this conference, but if that is the end of the questions, we shall bid you farewell and see you tomorrow. Thank you," I said, closing out the interview with the press.

Octavia

The next morning, when I awoke, I looked on the nightstand and saw the pregnancy test Athena had given me. Looking at Jensen lying there in bed, asleep, I grabbed the test and went into the bathroom. I looked at it and wondered, "Could it be true, and if in fact it is, do I keep it a secret til I see a doctor?" As soon as I was done following the directions of the test, I set it on the edge of the sink and waited.

"Babe, are you in here?" a voice asked as the door opened. "Are you all right?" Jensen asked, seeing me leaning against the sink.

"I'm fine. I was just thinking," I said, quickly grabbing the test off the counter.

"Thinking about what, beautiful?" Jensen said, kissing me.

"Just everything. Us, the band, you name it—all kinds of good stuff."

"Well, at least it's all good stuff. I'm going to jump in the shower. You want to join me?"

"Maybe in a minute," I said, kissing him back and walking out of the bathroom.

When I heard the sound of the shower, I grasped the test in my hand and thought about what I would tell my parents if the test came out positive. Not giving any thought to what Athena said about the child being important to the future, opening my hand, I looked at the test.

One Last Lesson

Jensen Kane

As the day faded away, the night came with heavy clouds covering the moon. Mentally preparing ourselves for the concert to come, we celebrated our success and how far we'd come and how we couldn't have done it without each other.

"Guys, this is just the beginning. We've come so far in so little time, and I'm so proud to say we're not only a band but a family. Let's make this a night never to forget and show our troops out there just how much we appreciate them," Octavia said, putting her hand out like we were in a huddle.

"Hell yeah!" Connor shouted as we all shouted "Embrace the Fate" together.

"Dean, Jensen, come here for a second. I want to talk to the both of you," Nathaniel said as we walked over to him before going on stage. "Listen, boys, I want you to stay alert out there. Have fun but remain vigilant and steadfast."

"Dad, everything's going to be fine. We'll do as you say and stay alert and watch out for each other," I said, assuring Nathaniel that we would all stay steadfast. "I promise."

"That's all I ask," Nathaniel said.

"Your father and I are going to be out there in the crowd to help with security and keep an eye out for anything unusual," Maya said, hugging us. "Now, you guys, get out there and have fun," she said smiling.

When we walked out on the stage, it was dark with just enough light for us to see where we were going. Dean walked to his drums while Connor and I found our places. Walking up to my synthesizer, I looked out at the crowd. They were patient but had that fire in their eyes, ready to rock. Octavia took a deep breath and touched her stomach before walking out on stage. The lights beamed down on her, and I began playing softly while the troops went crazy at the sight of Octavia. Walking up to her microphone, she adjusted it and turned looking at me, giving me a smile that I've only seen on rare occasions. I sensed her to be super excited about something, but about what, I didn't know. She had been quiet most of the day, keeping her focus on a book she was reading. I smiled back at her, and she continued to adjust her microphone and turned and looked at Dean, nodding. Dean tapped his sticks together, counting us off. We held a strong beat, and Octavia began head-banging. This was something I'd never seen her do before, but she did it well.

Octavia sings/metal sound:
The sultan I once was
No one could touch me, but you
Destiny's bound us
And then I betrayed you
Destiny's razors
The angels just stood by and laughed
No matter the sinful thoughts
We were as two flowers in my thoughts
Too paradise
Our pleasures go deep
Our hearts will fly free

Octavia sings/metal sound:
The sins I did
I did within
The desires within
The burning desires
I tried to defy them
Forgive my sins

Octavia sings/metal sound:
I am the sultan
You're amongst the sins I've burned
Lost is how I was created
And now I'm discovering
In paradise I sleep
My pleasures go deep
My heart flies free

Octavia sings/metal sound/chorus:
The sins I did
I did within
The desires within
The burning desires
I tried to defy them
Forgive my sins

Octavia sings/metal sound:
Trust me, oh trust me
I can fly and take you with me
Our love must come with us
We'll know the pleasures of sinners
Our hearts will fly free

[*Repeat chorus*]

As the song ended, I looked out at the crowd and saw four people that had not been there before standing completely still. They were dressed in black with charcoal-gray cloaks hiding their faces. Their bright eyes pierced through the darkness, fixated on Octavia. Of the four of them, one was a woman. She was about five-nine, 125 pounds. I could see her black hair coming out from the sides of the hood. The four of them split apart, still keeping their gaze locked on Octavia. I noticed that when they moved, they drew no attention to themselves, and they appeared to glide rather than walk like wraiths waiting for an opportune moment to strike.

I led us into the next song playing the synthesizer softly when I noticed that Nathaniel and Maya both had their eyes on the hooded figures. Suddenly without warning, I saw the female unveil herself, showing her face. She was beautiful. Her skin color was pale but healthy, and her long black hair was sinister as it floated mysteriously around her. Flicking her wrist, a katana appeared, and she jumped onto the stage. Immediately drawing the Nevillin, I blocked her katana from hitting Octavia. The troops cheered as they thought this to be part of the show. When the light of the moon vanished, shadows began falling from the sky, and Jinn began appearing everywhere.

"Men, we're under attack!" a soldier shouted out as he grabbed his sidearm and riddled one of the Jinn with bullets.

"Octavia, get behind me!" I shouted as the girl glared at Dean and Connor.

All of a sudden, another one of the hooded creatures jumped on the stage and lunged at Dean. Dean flicked his wrist, and when his spear appeared, he immediately deflected the blows and plunged his spear through the creature's chest. Looking to Connor, I could see that he was outmatched as he fought hard to take on a Jinn that attacked him. Taking his guitar, he went to hit the Jinn. The Jinn blocked it with its arm, and it shattered into pieces. The Jinn hit Connor in the chest, sending him flying up against one of the speakers on stage.

"Spraygin, give me the Christ bitch, and take your place by my side," the girl demanded as the troops in the crowd ran for cover.

"Who the hell are you?" I asked.

"We could be a family again, you, me . . . Mom," the girl said.

"Mom?" I asked. "You must be mistaken."

"You're Spraygin, the son of Everin Goodwater, princess of heaven, are you not?" the girl asked, confused, keeping her katana pointed at me.

"Everin Goodwater, what do you know of Everin Goodwater?"

"Enough."

"Then you must know she died in the war in heaven."

"Is that what you've been told?" the girl asked angry.

"Who are you?"

"Your sister," the girl said, staring at Octavia and I. "Your twin sister. My name is Rayne."

I looked out into the crowd and saw my mother and father fighting a hooded figure. The katana it was wielding had a lot of curvature in the blade and had blue fire flowing all over it. It was beautiful, like nothing I'd ever seen before.

"They're dead. Spraygin, you can't help them, but you can help yourself. Give me the Elder Grimoire and let me carve that disease out of your girlfriend, and I'll take you away from here. I'll take you home," Rayne said before swinging her katana at Octavia only to be blocked by Nathaniel.

"We meet again."

"And you are?" Nathaniel asked, holding the Rayne's katana in place.

"I'm sure you already know the answer to that," Rayne said, staring deep into Nathaniel's eyes. "It figures you wouldn't recognize your own daughter."

"Daughter?" Nathaniel looked, confused.

Suddenly Jinn were flying at us from all directions. They were fixed on Nathaniel and came at him with everything they had, pushing him away from Rayne. Fighting the Jinn off him, I kicked Rayne to the ground. Lifting my katana, I went for a shot to kill Rayne.

"Don't you dare lay a finger on her, Spraygin!" the demonic creature said, holding its blue fire katana to Nathaniel's back while still hidden behind the hooded cloak.

When all the fighting stopped around us, Maya, Dean, and Connor all looked on in fear and desperation.

"If I let her go, what guarantee do I have that you're not going to harm him?"

"None," it said, pressing its katana up against Nathaniel's back a little harder.

"Don't you drop your katana, Jensen," Nathaniel said sternly.

"You harm him, and I'll really give you a reason to hide your face."

"Such threats. Now, let her go, or I'll run him through," it said as Nathaniel squinted and grinned his teeth.

"All right!" I shouted, letting Rayne go. "Now release him."

"No problem," it said as it drove its katana through Nathaniel's back, coming out the front.

"No!" Maya shouted, screaming as it ripped its katana out from his back, and Nathaniel fell to his knees.

"Consider him released," it mocked as I lunged at Rayne and it.

I never fought so hard in my life. I went at it with everything I had till I kicked Rayne to the ground and swung at it, making contact with its face.

"Roquin," Maya said in terror and shock as Roquin stood there bleeding, and his hood was no longer in place. "Why, why are you doing this?"

"If only you knew what I know, Maya," Roquin said. He flicked his wrist, and a portal opened behind him where I saw another shadowy figure standing in the distance.

The portal was dark and cloudy and appeared in the shape of a doorway. Swinging the Nevillin one last time, I fought Rayne but she wasn't as skilled as I, swinging the Nevillin I made contact with the right side of her neck. Falling to her knees, the portal closed. With a swift kick and punch, Roquin defended Rayne and sent Maya and I flying into separate directions. Looking over at my mom, we both became bombarded by Jinn attacking us. I could see from a distance Dean was keeping Octavia safe and fighting off Jinn. Suddenly, the cleaver of a Jinn pierced into Maya's right shoulder. Pulling it out, it raised its weapon in the air.

"I don't think so," Dean said, furiously blocking the Jinn's cleaver as it swung to kill Maya.

Dean pushed the Jinn back and grasped his spear. Driving it through the Jinn, it let out a roar and grabbed Dean, punching him in the face till he was limp and bleeding. Fighting the Jinn off myself, I saw Roquin crouch down, making eye contact with Nathaniel.

"And God called you his champion," Roquin mocked. "Look at you now."

"You can't win this, Roquin. Jensen's stronger than you," Nathaniel said, breathing heavily.

"Let me ask you, does he know who his father is, Nathaniel?" Roquin said, sharply staring into Nathaniel's eyes. "I used to look at Everin with such lust. Until I finally bared my soul to her, only to have it rejected. Thrown into my face, and find out you and she were together in more ways than one."

"You did this out of jealousy?" Nathaniel asked, chuckling and coughing.

"Don't patronize me, Nathaniel. It was you she loved more than anyone," Roquin said in a jealous rage. "Did Lucifer or Maya know of you two and your betrayal? Probably not, right? What a champion. You with all your secrets," Roquin sneered. "You're no different than me, Nathaniel, and I must say, I'm quite disappointed. Nonetheless, I see the resemblance of Everin and you in them, and it makes the skin crawl off my bones."

"What are you talking about?" Nathaniel asked confused.

"You don't know?" Roquin sinisterly laughed. "Here at your end, you learn the truth."

"What truth?"

"Jensen and Rayne. They look an awful lot like you." Roquin smiled. "Every time I saw you and Everin together, I kept my mouth shut. We are more like the humans than we ever thought, sneaking around doing naughty things behind the backs of the ones we say we love."

"You tried to kill them?" Nathaniel asked as blood ran from his nose and out the side of his mouth. "Before they were even born. It was you who took Rayne."

"Yes, but then that Christ bitch got involved, and we know what happened after that. But enough with the history lesson."

Standing up, Roquin gripped his katana and went to drive it through Nathaniel one last time. Flying through all the Jinn in my path, I blocked Roquin's katana, and in one smooth motion, I severed both his hands at the wrists. Dropping his katana to the ground, he let out a violent scream.

"You!" Roquin said, breathing heavily.

"Disappointed?" I asked, staying steadfast.

"Not in the least!" Roquin said before I ran the Nevillin through his body.

"Now it's over," I said, staring at him as he fell to the ground and slowly disappeared.

Then from out of nowhere, a shadow fell from the sky, another hooded figure with unmatched strength. I attempted to fight it. It grabbed me, lifting me into the air, pummeling me with its fists until I was breathing shallow and coughing up blood. It threw me to the ground. Picking up Rayne, it flew back into the sky, and all the Jinn followed.

"Jensen!" Octavia shouted, running to my side.

"Nathaniel," I said in a shallow breath. "Where's Nathaniel?"

"Come, Jensen," Octavia said, helping me to my feet.

"Nathaniel," I said, looking at him lying there on the ground while Maya held his hand and Dean and Connor looked on in sadness.

"Jensen, the katana," Nathaniel said, fading in and out of consciousness. "Roquin's katana. Bring it to me," Nathaniel said as Dean handed me Roquin's katana.

As soon as I grasped it, it disappeared, and a tattoo of an angelic sigil appeared on my forearm. It was the angelic sigil of Roquin.

"Wherever he is, he's gone now. You hold his katana. Now, take this. Keep it safe," Nathaniel said, handing me the Elder Grimoire.

"I will."

"And you," he said, looking at Octavia. "I know of the excitement you feel about the baby growing inside you. She, without a doubt, is very special and will change the world."

"It's a girl?" Octavia said, smiling.

"You're pregnant?" I asked, shocked.

"Jensen, Maya," Nathaniel coughed. "I must tell you something."

"You don't have to say anything, my love. I know everything," Maya said, beginning to cry. "I always have. I loved you too much to ever care, and I forgive you."

"I'm sorry I wronged you," Nathaniel said as tears flowed from his eyes. "I love you, Maya."

"Jensen, I want you to take this now," Nathaniel said, flicking his wrist. "It's the katana of Godric Goodwater. You must show it to all the troops here. Once you do this, the evil of this night will be erased from their memories. When the time comes, the katana will leave you and return to its rightful owner," Nathaniel said, gasping for air.

"How do you know this, Dad?"

"Godric told me."

"We have to get him to a hospital!" I shouted.

"I'm done, Jensen. No hospitals. I've poured everything of myself into you, son. From now on, when you fight, my spirit fights beside you. I've taught you countless lessons except one," Nathaniel said, holding Maya's hand tight as she cried. "It's time you learn to let go," Nathaniel said, breathing heavily. "This is the one lesson I couldn't teach you in life, but it's the one last lesson I can teach you from my death."

"I'll miss you every day," I said as I laid my head on his chest, sobbing. "I love you," I said, taking the katana of Godric Goodwater from his hand. "Nathaniel Kane, my true father," I whispered as he closed his eyes and his body slowly vanished and his katana remained. Taking his katana in my hand I flicked my wrist and Nathaniel's angelic sigil appeared on my arm above Roquin's. As the troops looked on in sadness, I raised the katana of Godic Goodwater in the air and told my family to look away.

The End

About the Author

Timothy Aberle was born in Las Vegas, Nevada. At the age of eight, his family migrated to Dana Point, California. Growing up with two brothers, he learned the importance of friendship and loyalty. Regularly attending Saint Edwards Catholic Church with his family, he developed a strong interest in religion and decided to research as many different religions as possible throughout his years.

Having an eccentric imagination, he drew inspiration through different genres of music and adventurous movies. Growing up on the beaches of Strands and Salt Creek, he grew a deep respect and love for the ocean. His love for the ocean fueled his imagination and daydreaming about the unknown became normal. While others found surfing and boogie boarding to be great pastimes, Timothy often wrote short stories and songs in a journal and spent much of his time at the local library reading

Stephen King books. It wasn't till he attended Dana Hills High School that Timothy enrolled himself in a bible literature class in search of further educating himself on religion. At this time, he penned a short story called Cain's Fury as a project for class and received high praise for its creativity.

A big turning point in Timothy's life was when his mother, Donna, fell ill to a rare deadly disease called scleroderma. His mother stricken with grief, desperately turned to reading inspirational books about Angels to help cope with the stress of being sick. Through chemotherapy and heart wrenching times, Timothy witnessed the courage of both his mother and father. On October 3rd, 1999 tragedy fell over Timothy's household when his beloved mother, Donna, passed away.

Moving back to Las Vegas to start over, Timothy fell in love with a young lady with a love for books. After sharing his short story, Cain's Fury, with the young lady who he would soon marry, she encouraged him to allow his imagination to go to work and he began writing his debut novel. Using Cain's Fury as the template, **Chronicles of Kane** was born.

Timothy resides in Las Vegas with his wife and two children, Dean and Sam. He works for a luxury home builder as a service technician and remains hard at work on **Legacy of Kane**, the next volume in the Kane trilogy.

www.ingramcontent.com/pod-product-compliance
Lightning Source LLC
Chambersburg PA
CBHW030631190726
48286CB00008B/2479